STRAWBERRY

And Other Short Stories

SURESH HEGDE

STARDOM BOOKS

www.StardomBooks.com

STARDOM BOOKS
112 Bordeaux Ct.
Coppell, TX 75019, USA

FIRST EDITION FEBRUARY 2025

STARDOM BOOKS, LLC.
112 Bordeaux Ct. Coppell, TX 75019, USA

www.stardombooks.com

Stardom Books, United States
Stardom Alliance, India

STRAWBERRY
And Other Short Stories

Suresh Hegde

p. 146
cm. 13.97 X 21.59

Category:
FIC029000 Fiction: Short Stories (single author)

ISBN: 978-1-957456-68-3

DEDICATION

I dedicate this book to all the members of my family for their love and support.

CONTENTS

ACKNOWLEDGMENTS

My sincere acknowledgments are due to Shri Arunkumar Habbu, Senior Journalist, Hubli, who helped me translate the stories to English.
My son, Ravichandra Hegde, who has been instrumental in bringing out the English version of my book. My family members for their encouragement.
My sincere thanks to Shree Monappa, Senior Artist for the beautiful Cover Page
The management of Stardom Books for publishing my book.

1

THE PSALM OF LIFE

Sudhakar was lost in thought. What was he thinking about?

It was about Ashok! Out of the blue, Ashok had sent Sudhakar a message, writing to him after many years. All this while, Sudhakar had been reminiscing about the good old days, especially about something that had puzzled him for years. He was surprised to realize that all the questions lingering in his mind from those days were still vivid and resurfaced the moment he read his friend's message.

"Dear Sudhakar," Ashok wrote, "I will be pleased to welcome you and your family to stay with us for a while. Here are the Flight tickets. Waiting to see you, my friend."

Sudhakar's mind became a whirlwind of emotions. He was overjoyed at the thought of meeting his friend, who had once been like family, after such a long time. Yet, he felt anxious about the reason for the invitation, wondering why Ashok had asked for his entire family to visit. He hoped everything was alright.

Lost in thought, Sudhakar was startled by a nudge on his shoulder. It was his wife, Rohini. Seeing her husband so preoccupied, Rohini asked, "Why don't you just call Ashok and find out why he wants us over instead of worrying?" However, Sudhakar shook his head and replied, "No." He still couldn't decide what to do.

The days passed quickly, and on the eve of their departure, Sudhakar voiced his discomfort to Rohini. "Ashok still hasn't told me why he wants us to visit. You know me, Rohini. I don't like being kept in the dark. But since he's gone to the extent of booking flight tickets for all three of us, we really have to go. It wouldn't look good if we declined his invitation at this point. Let's get ready to leave for Delhi tomorrow."

Rohini agreed with her husband; she, too, felt visiting Ashok was the right thing to do. Sudhakar, Rohini, and their daughter Jhanavi began packing their bags. As planned, the family boarded an Indigo flight from Hubli and arrived at the Delhi domestic airport.

Throughout the journey, Sudhakar was still lost in his thoughts. He kept reminiscing about how he first met Ashok and how they had drifted apart over time. He wondered if he could have kept in touch with Ashok like in the old days. But could things ever go back to being the same? Can someone truly change their perception of another, even when they know their real nature? Staring out the airplane window at the fluffy, white clouds, Sudhakar found his own thoughts clouded and confusing—unlike the clarity of the sky outside.

At the airport, Sudhakar, Rohini, and Jhanavi retrieved their luggage from the tenth conveyor belt and walked toward the exit doors. It felt like a scene from a movie as they saw a line of taxi drivers waving placards, waiting to collect their passengers. While they stood at the main gate, a young boy waved enthusiastically at them, shouting, "Hello, Uncle! Over here!"

The family walked toward the boy, who turned out to be Vivek, Ashok's son. Being the polite and traditional boy he was, Vivek took the luggage trolley from Sudhakar's hands, sought the couple's blessings, and exchanged greetings with Jhanavi. He then led them to his Skoda Rapid parked nearby.

As Vivek loaded the bags into the car, Sudhakar observed him closely and realized how much Vivek resembled his father. "Such a handsome young man," Sudhakar thought. "He's a spitting image of Ashok. His neatly styled hair, the dimple on his right cheek when he smiles, and his sharp eyes behind those sunglasses—all of it reminds me of Ashok. One look at this boy, and anyone could tell he's intelligent and talented."

Vivek drove Sudhakar and his family to Ashok's residence. The sun was setting, painting the wide, empty roads with a pale orange hue. The sky was clear, with no dark clouds in sight. Inside the car, a pleasant aroma lingered, complemented by Talat Aziz's ghazal "Woh Shaam Bhala Ab Kyu Yaadon Se Nahi Jaati" playing softly in the background. The ride was comfortable for everyone.

Breaking the silence, Vivek initiated the conversation. "So, what else is new, Uncle? How are things in Hubli? I can never forget the mouth-watering treats from Hubli, especially Girmit." Vivek had visited Hubli a couple of years earlier when he was in his final year of MBA.

He had traveled to Hubli to collect his amended birth certificate from the municipal corporation, a document required for his passport issuance. Sudhakar had helped Vivek get the work done quickly through an acquaintance, enabling him to complete the process in just two days. During his stay in Hubli, Vivek grew very close to Sudhakar's family. He even gave useful academic tips to Jhanavi, who was then in her fifth year at Hubli's BVB Engineering College.

Recalling his visit, Vivek turned to Rohini and said, "Aunty, I still remember the white pearl onion curry you made when I visited. Could you make it again while you're here? Please?" Rohini, delighted by Vivek's request, immediately agreed. "Oh yes, of course! Why not?"

Sudhakar, on the other hand, couldn't stop observing Vivek. He marveled at how well-groomed and refined Vivek had become in just ur years. Finally, Sudhakar said, "Vivek, you didn't have to come all the way to pick us up. We could have just taken a cab." To this, Vivek replied politely, "Arrey, Uncle, not at all. Saturdays are a holiday anyway. Plus, you have no idea how eagerly your friend is waiting for you back home. Oh, that reminds me—let me call my dad and let him know we're on our way."

Vivek made the call. "Hello, Dad? Yes, the flight was on time. We're on our way and have just crossed the central market." The four continued the rest of the journey in comfortable silence, enjoying the music and the view.

They finally arrived at Ashok's residence. The house was a four-bedroom bungalow located on Narayan Road in Ashok Vihar. Adjacent to the famous Nidhi Plaza, it was situated in the well-developed Vishal Park area. A beautiful park lay right in front of the house, featuring a granite slab at its center where people often gathered to relax and converse. On the wall outside the bungalow hung a board that read, "Dr. Kathyayini S, Delhi University."

Ashok, who had been restlessly waiting at the doorstep, rushed out as soon as the car arrived. He embraced Sudhakar warmly and said, "I'm so happy to see you, Sudhakar! Rohini, it's great to see you, and Jhanavi, so glad you're here, kid."

While they exchanged pleasantries, Vivek carried all their bags into the guest room. Everyone settled in, and Ashok eagerly asked Sudhakar, in a Yakshagana style, "May I ask what tasty snacks Sudhakar has brought along for his Kuchela?"

Rohini quickly replied, "We've got plenty," and opened boxes filled with Babu Singh Pedha, Savanur Mix, Holige, Kunda from Belgaum, and a variety of other sweets and snacks.

Time flew, and evening arrived. Vivek mentioned that Ashok's sister, Kathyayini, would soon join them to enjoy the treats.

Rohini and Sudhakar finished their tour of the house and sat down. Sudhakar couldn't help but wonder how only three people resided in such a large house. After retiring, Ashok had been nominated by the central government as an advisor to the Environmental Institution, a position he had held for the past three years. Kathyayini, his sister, was the Head of the English Department at Delhi University, while Vivek, the dynamic young man, worked as a top executive at the Sapient company in Noida, just thirty kilometers from Delhi. Ashok employed several staff members to manage household chores, including Bhayya Harilal, their favorite cook, who hailed from Uttar Pradesh.

As Sudhakar strolled around the house, Ashok shadowed him closely, almost like a pet cat, never leaving his side. Observing this, Sudhakar asked, "Ashokji, is everything alright with you? It seems Sharadakka's demise has affected you deeply. Are you okay?"

"You're right, Sudhakar," Ashok replied with a heavy heart. "I still can't come to terms with the fact that Sharada is no longer with us. I feel a mix of mental agony, desperation, and regret all at once. It's truly difficult to cope with these emotions. I rarely spent time with her when I was working; I was always roaming the forests. I had hoped to spend quality time with her after retirement, but... destiny had other plans. I wasn't fortunate enough to have that time with her."

Sudhakar had visited Ashok on the day of his retirement, following 35 years of service as Deputy Conservator of Forests in Karwar. The entire district forest department had gathered to honor his contributions, and everyone was emotional about bidding him farewell. The Conservator of Forests from Bengaluru and several environmentalists attended as special guests, adding grandeur to the occasion.

Addressing the somber gathering, Ashok had shared his deep concerns about the rapid depletion of forest reserves due to selfish human activities masquerading as development.

"Yes, I am deeply worried and pained," he had said in a grave voice. "The lush green reserves of the Western Ghats and the beloved Arabian Sea coast, cherished by Rabindranath Tagore, are fading into history. I had shared this agony with my close friend Sudhakar long ago."

In truth, Ashok hadn't been happy on his retirement day. His wife, Sharada, had been bedridden for a week at the time. A well-known cardiologist, Dr. Heggadekatte, had informed Ashok that her condition was critical and that she might not have much time left. Tragically, Sharadakka passed away a week later due to congestive cardiac arrest.

Sudhakar and Ashok were lost in their memories when Kathyayini joined them. It had been years since Sudhakar had last seen her, and she had visibly aged. Her mature demeanor reflected the passage of time. Yet, Kathyayini was thrilled to see Sudhakar and his family and greeted them with infectious enthusiasm.

Without wasting any time, she eagerly asked about her share of the snacks. As she munched on the delicious treats from Hubli, Kathyayini fondly reminisced about her childhood days.

That evening, both families enjoyed a sumptuous dinner of Uttar Pradesh delicacies prepared by Harilal. The table was laden with dishes like Batti Choka, Bedhai Tehri, Bhendi Salan, and many more. For Sudhakar and Rohini, it was a unique and delightful experience, while Jhanavi, tired of the monotonous food at her PG, savored every bite. She worked as a Programme Engineer at Oracle and cherished this refreshing change.

The lively conversation continued late into the night, with laughter and nostalgia filling the air. Suddenly, a loud sound interrupted the chatter. Everyone turned to see Ashok standing with his glass, having struck it to grab their attention. He had succeeded.

"From tomorrow, Mrs. Rohini will be taking over our kitchen. With Harilal's assistance, Mrs. Rohini will cook us traditional North Kanara dishes like huli, tambuli, gojju, payasam, kadabu, tellevu, and more," declared Ashok, sounding as if he were making a formal business announcement. As soon as Ashok finished, Kathyayini and Vivek enthusiastically joined in, thumping the table and cheering, "Yes... Yes!" Rohini smiled and nodded in agreement, indicating she would be delighted to take on the task.

While everyone enjoyed the lighthearted moment, Sudhakar once again drifted into his thoughts. He marveled at how fond Ashok had become of him. Ashok had gone to the extent of booking flight tickets for Sudhakar, Rohini, and Jhanavi in advance, without even informing them, insisting they come and enjoy a short vacation in Delhi. Yet, amidst these cheerful musings, doubts began to creep into Sudhakar's mind. Memories from the past that made him uneasy resurfaced, casting a shadow over his mood. Just a moment ago, he had been reveling in Ashok's company, and now he was recalling the day when he first began doubting Ashok's loyalty.

Over the years, Ashok had become more than a friend to Sudhakar; he was like an elder brother, someone Sudhakar deeply respected. Ashok was known for his resolute nature—once he made a decision, he rarely wavered. Even during Sharadakka's passing, Ashok had taken charge and made all the decisions about her last rites on his own. Only a handful of people attended the funeral—a small circle of colleagues and a few neighbors. None of Sharadakka's family members were present. Her only brother, who once lived in Sainagar, Hubli, had moved to America. Even Kathyayini was unable to travel from Delhi in time.

Ashok had performed the last rites himself. He bathed his wife's body, dressed her in a new saree, and adorned her mortal remains with flowers and sindhur. He even asked his son Vivek to place a sandalwood garland on her. In the end, he donated her body to KIMS (Karnataka Institute of Medical Sciences). When people questioned his actions, Ashok explained that this was a mutual decision he and Sharadakka had made long ago.

Though Ashok appeared composed outwardly, the truth was far from it. He mourned deeply, often sitting under a tree, weeping for his wife. On the 13th day, Ashok and Vivek traveled to Trayambakeshwar to complete the final rituals.

As Sudhakar dwelled on these memories, the lively chatter of the gathering pulled him back to the present. Both families continued their conversations late into the night. Eventually, Ashok noticed Sudhakar's drowsy eyes and decided to wrap up the evening.

"Ah! You must be exhausted from the journey. I'll let you rest now. Good night!" Ashok said as he switched off the lights and gently closed the door behind him.

Sudhakar, lying in bed, tried to sleep but found himself lost in a sea of memories. His mind drifted to the past, to the day he first met Ashok. After completing his graduation, Sudhakar had taken up a job in Mumbai. However, he longed to move closer to his parents and find work in his district. Fortune smiled on him when he secured a position with the Kali Project, which had just been launched in Supa.

Although Supa was in the same district, Sudhakar had to rely on a map to locate the remote, godforsaken place. The small town was steeped in mythology, believed to have been the dwelling of Shurpanakha from the Ramayana, and it was named Supa after her. Nestled in the heart of a lush, green forest, Supa was designated as a Taluk by the Revenue Department. It housed a taluk office, a police station, a post office, a health center, a government school, and a forest department office dedicated to conserving the region's rich forest reserves.

Although Supa had basic facilities, many government officials avoided their duties there to escape the dreadful malaria and heavy rainfall. The majority of Supa's residents spoke Konkani, while others used a mix of Marathi and Konkani. Consequently, many referred to the Kannada language as "Kaanadi." Public transportation in Supa was limited to a bus route from Belgaum via Supa and another from Sadashivagad to Supa. Sudhakar's posting required him to report to the isolated village of Virkhol, about two kilometers from Supa.

Since the office had only recently been established, Sudhakar and his teammates lacked a proper office building. Instead, they worked out of a dilapidated iron shed, once used by miners, which served as their temporary workspace. This makeshift office was located in the small village of Virkhol.

The Kali River, originating in Diggi near Karwar, flowed for approximately 160 kilometers before merging with the Arabian Sea. Along its journey, the river and its tributaries, Pandari and Judu, nurtured rich flora and fauna. However, hydroelectric projects along the river had disrupted this natural beauty. Sudhakar's role involved protecting the environment, assisting with the rehabilitation of displaced residents, and proposing alternative methods for forest conservation.

Finding shelter in such an isolated village proved to be a challenge. Coming from the comfort of his sister's home in Mumbai, Sudhakar initially felt disappointed with the lack of basic civic amenities in Virkhol. There were moments when he regretted his decision to leave his well-paying job. However, the opportunity to visit his parents frequently and the satisfaction of serving his district lifted his spirits, providing the motivation he needed to endure his time in Supa.

Eventually, Sudhakar found a place to stay. The house, with its simple Kadapa flooring, lacked modern amenities, including a lavatory. At night, he managed with the light of a lantern. The rent was a mere five rupees per month. Despite these hardships, Sudhakar found solace in the surrounding lush green forests and the serene Kali River. His neighbors, who were also government officials, offered a sense of community. Over time, Sudhakar adjusted and began to settle into his new life.

One day, during duty hours, Sudhakar noticed a tall and sturdy man speeding past on a Bullet motorcycle down the lane near his house. The man turned out to be Range Forest Officer Ashok, whom Sudhakar had first met when visiting the project office to gather information about the extent of forestland that would be submerged by the project. What began as a professional relationship gradually developed into a deep friendship. Their frequent encounters, from one end of the colony to another, helped Sudhakar overcome his boredom and loneliness.

Sudhakar developed a profound emotional bond with Ashok's family—his wife, Sharadakka, and their son, Vivek. He became an integral part of their lives. Weekends were often spent playing chess, carrom, and other games with Vivek, followed by lunch or dinner at Ashok's house.

Sudhakar also accompanied Ashok on routine visits to the lush forests, relishing the melodious chirping of birds, the roars of cheetahs, and the sight of jumping deer, antelopes, and hooting jackals. Ashok always carried his Canon camera slung over his shoulder, never missing an opportunity to capture the wilderness. Anyone who knew Ashok could attest to his passion for his work. For Ashok, his profession was more than just a job; it was a calling. He couldn't bear to see even a single scratch on the trees or harm to their inhabitants.

As the two walked through the forest one day, Ashok turned to Sudhakar and began a conversation.

"Sudhakar, forests are the homes of wild animals. No one has the right to destroy their homes. Humans are so selfish; all they think about is their own material gains. Where will these wild animals go? With no shelter, they start invading human habitats. This friction between humans and animals is dangerous. It is undoubtedly a sign of annihilation. I get anxious just thinking about it," said Ashok passionately.

That day had not been easy for Ashok. He had received calls from higher-ups in Anashi village and had to arrange accommodations for several officials. From early morning, he had been working tirelessly in the field and was required to spend the night outside. In his absence, a forest guard was assigned to look after Ashok's house for the day.

After their forest visit, Sudhakar returned home, exhausted from the walk, and fell asleep early. Around midnight, a loud banging at his door startled him awake. The banging continued persistently. Terrified, Sudhakar rushed to open the door.

At the door stood the forest guard, frightened and gasping for breath. Once he managed to catch his breath, the guard informed Sudhakar, "Sir, you need to come with me immediately. Saheb's son Vivek is struggling to breathe. It looks very serious. Please, he needs your help!"

Horrified, Sudhakar wasted no time and ran toward Ashok's house. Vivek lay there, pale and gasping for air. Despite his usual composure, the sight of Vivek in such a state overwhelmed Sudhakar with emotion, bringing tears to his eyes. However, he quickly realized the gravity of the situation and called his colleague in Mamadapur for assistance. Without hesitation, Sudhakar carried Vivek to Dr. Kamath's clinic in Dandeli, accompanied by Sharadakka.

At the clinic, the doctor immediately began running tests on Vivek while Sudhakar and Sharadakka anxiously waited outside. After what felt like an eternity, Dr. Kamath called them in and said, "Vivek seems to have contracted diphtheria. He exhibits all the symptoms. You did well to bring him in on time; you've saved his life."

Dr. Kamath treated Vivek with utmost care, and soon the young boy was out of danger. This incident brought Sudhakar even closer to Ashok and his family. Days passed, and Vivek gradually regained his health, returning to his usual cheerful self.

One day, Ashok invited Sudhakar and urged him to bring his parents to Supa for a visit. Ashok wanted to host them and spend quality time with them. Initially, Sudhakar politely declined the invitation, but Ashok's persistence eventually convinced him. When Sudhakar's parents arrived in Supa, they had a delightful stay with their son and Ashok's family. Ashok was particularly impressed by how Sudhakar cared for his parents and the warmth they shared.

Despite Sudhakar's growing closeness with Ashok's family, he knew little about Ashok's own parents or his ancestral background. Sudhakar never asked, and Ashok never shared—until one evening. During a visit to the British Tourist Bungalow, Ashok opened up and shared his family history with Sudhakar.

Ashok belonged to Sode, a village in the North Kanara district, located on the banks of the Shalmala River. The region, once ruled by King Sadashiv Raya II, was lush with greenery and enveloped by forests. The air was fresh and inviting, offering a sense of tranquility.

King Sadashiv Raya II had skillfully utilized the region's natural resources—water, land, and flora—to construct a majestic fort. This fort was known by various names: Giri Durga (Fort on a Hill), Vana Durga (Fort in a Forest), and Nela Durga (Fort of the Land). At the main gate of the fort stood two beautiful temples dedicated to

Huliyappa (the God of Tigers) and Lord Hanuman. Ashok's ancestors served as the appointed priests of these temples.

Priests were held in high regard in those days, and as a mark of respect, the King had granted Ashok's ancestors a piece of land. However, as time passed and the kingdom fell into decline, Ashok's family transitioned to agriculture and other occupations to sustain themselves.

Ashok's grandfather was addicted to various drugs, and one day, he abandoned Ashok's mother, Ahalye, and left town. Ahalye, a young woman in her prime, faced unimaginable struggles being alone and without family support. She was subjected to harassment by many men with evil intentions. In the end, Ahalye gave in and became Shivappa Nayaka's mistress to escape the greedy eyes preying on her vulnerability.

Ahalye and Shivappa Nayaka had two children: Ashok and his sister, Kathyayini. Ashok stayed under Nayaka's care until he could make decisions for himself, and then he left home to seek refuge at the Ramakrishna Ashrama in Mysuru. Ashok completed his education while staying and volunteering at the ashram. That night, as Ashok shared his past, he could not hold back his emotions. On the other hand, Sudhakar patiently listened to every word, watching tears stream down Ashok's cheeks.

"You and your parents share a beautiful bond, Sudhakar. To be honest, I envy you. I wish I could have experienced such love as a boy. I'm born a sinner," Ashok said, sobbing uncontrollably.

Ashok had consumed a considerable amount of whiskey that night and was gradually losing awareness of his surroundings. Understanding Ashok's fragile mental state, Sudhakar helped him up and took him to his cottage.

Ashok often brought Sudhakar to public gatherings, introducing him as his close friend. Although Ashok was a student of Botany, he had a deep love for English literature. Kurandi Mines' partner, Ayyangar, would bring him loads of English novels during visits to Bengaluru. Ashok and Ayyangar would sit together at the

Kumbarvada camp, enjoying these novels with a couple of pegs of Old Monk.

Ashok's mother, in her old age, lived with him while Kathyayini stayed in Dharwad, pursuing her education. However, Ashok's mother didn't live long; she passed away while Ashok was posted in Ankola. Kathyayini often visited Ashok in Supa, and whenever she met Sudhakar, she would proudly recount her university days, much to Ashok's irritation. Ashok had once confided in Sudhakar about Kathyayini's illicit relationship with Prof. Panchamukhi, expressing his shame and disapproval.

Certain actions of Ashok began to unsettle Sudhakar, planting seeds of doubt in his mind. The most puzzling was Ashok's frequent visits to a village near Joida called Deriya. On these visits, Ashok would take Sudhakar along, accompanying a team of scientists studying the rapid extinction of species like the King Cobra and the Hornbill. However, each time they visited Deriya, Ashok would go into a specific house and return after 30 minutes or so. This pattern repeated itself on subsequent visits. Ashok would always say, "Wait here, Sudhakar. I'll be back soon," before disappearing into the house.

Unable to ignore his suspicions, Sudhakar began to believe Ashok was having an affair, especially since Sharadakka was unwell and unable to fulfill Ashok's physical needs. Though Sudhakar never confronted Ashok about his secretive activities, the doubts festered in his mind. Eventually, convinced of Ashok's unfaithfulness, Sudhakar began to distance himself emotionally.

Over time, both Sudhakar and Ashok were promoted to higher positions. Sudhakar married and settled with his family in Supa, while Ashok relocated to Khanapur and made it his home. Despite the physical distance and unspoken tensions, their friendship remained strong and enduring.

It had been nearly four days since Sudhakar and his family arrived in Delhi. Ashok had arranged for a taxi to make their sightseeing easier, enabling them to visit places like Agra, Qutub Minar, Red Fort, Akshardham Temple, India Gate, Rashtrapati Bhavan, and other must-see landmarks. Before their sightseeing trip, Rohini had prepared a delicious North Kanara traditional dinner, along with a special Kajjaya for the journey.

Harilal prepared and packed dahi, thepla, vangi bath, and other dishes for Sudhakar and his family for breakfast and lunch. Both families had set aside a day to explore Delhi's local markets for shopping. After breakfast, everyone set out for the adventure. Jhanavi traveled in Vivek's car while the rest of the group led the way in another vehicle.

They explored several iconic shopping streets, including Karol Bagh, Connaught Place, and Sarojini Market, to name a few. During their shopping spree, Ashok bought Sudhakar a kurta-pyjama set from FabIndia and a lehenga set for Jhanavi from Soch, with Vivek personally selecting the lehenga. "This is for you. I'm sure it will enhance your beauty," Vivek said, shaking Jhanavi's hand as he handed her the gift. Kathyayini joined the scene and added, "Let's hope we can become a family." Everyone smiled and nodded in agreement.

Jhanavi was a vibrant and lively young woman. Every morning, she would wake up and create colorful rangolis in front of the house. She had bonded exceptionally well with Ashok's family, so much so that she already felt like part of the family. One evening, as everyone sat outside chatting, Jhanavi brought a bottle of Parachute coconut oil and massaged Ashok's head, teasingly commenting that he needed to oil his hair more often. "You remind me of my mother, Jhanavi dear. Thank you," Ashok responded with tears in his eyes.

Vivek had also noticed the positive change in Ashok's demeanor since Sudhakar and his family's arrival. "Father is happy now, Uncle," Vivek remarked. "I haven't seen him this happy in years. Your visit has brought joy to his heart and brightened our home."

Sudhakar, too, observed these changes in Ashok. He noticed Ashok's growing indifference to external surroundings and his newfound interest in philosophical books. Ashok was often seen discussing various topics with Swami Raghuveeranandji of the Hubli Ramakrishna Ashram and environmentalists like Yellappa Reddy whenever he was in town. However, Sudhakar kept his thoughts to himself and refrained from making any comments.

Two days before Sudhakar and his family were set to depart, Ashok finally revealed the reason behind the sudden invitation to Delhi. As everyone gathered around the dining table, Ashok began to address them. He started by mentioning an event organized by his sister Kathyayini, titled Passage of Life, under the guidance of a senior professor from Delhi University. "I had an opportunity for introspection, and I wanted you to be a part of it, Sudhakar," he said, leaving Sudhakar curious and somewhat puzzled by Ashok's anxious and restless demeanor.

The Uttarayani Hall in Delhi's Chittaranjan Park was a breathtaking venue, worth the anticipation. It was adorned with colorful lights, and its pristine white interiors exuded a majestic aura. Half the seats in the hall were usually filled quickly, requiring attendees to arrive early to secure a good spot. The air was scented with the fragrance of Odonil Jasmine, and Praveen Godkindi's soulful flute recital of Raag Yaman played in the background, adding a serene touch to the atmosphere. The hall was graced by the presence of several renowned artists, and Kathyayini, along with her university group, was also present.

Sudhakar and Ashok arrived early and secured seats in the front row. The event began promptly, with Kathyayini being invited on stage to invoke divine blessings with a prayer. She sang a melodious hymn dedicated to Lord Ganesha, captivating the audience, and then addressed the gathering. Her flawless English and eloquence left Sudhakar in awe.

Following her introduction, Kathyayini invited Ashok to the stage. She spoke briefly about Ashok, highlighting his passion for environmental and wildlife protection and his notable contributions in the field. With that, she handed over the stage to Ashok, who was set to address the gathering.

Ashok had prepared a presentation showcasing the images of flora and fauna he had captured during his years of service. One of the slides featured a striking photograph of buffaloes, pigs, horses, and other animals bathing in muddy ponds, with a delicate lotus blooming in the corner. The image, a true picture worth a thousand words, left the audience intrigued, pondering its deeper meaning.

He also highlighted the splendor of the Western Ghats—its lush flora and fauna, breathtaking hilltops, sprawling areca nut gardens, towering coconut trees, and a variety of plants. The presentation earned him a torrent of admiration from the audience.

In the second half of the presentation, Ashok shifted focus to his personal life. He shared black-and-white photographs chronicling his time at the Ramakrishna Ashram in Mysuru, his graduation, his career in the forest department, his marital life, and the birth of his son, Vivek. All these cherished memories had been captured with his trusted Canon camera.

Pausing his presentation, Ashok gazed at the audience for a moment before speaking again. "I have something important to share," he began. "In the photographs you just saw, there is a moment when a remarkable person entered my life. When I was away for work, this man saved the light of my eyes—my son. He is a true blessing in my life." Ashok then gestured toward Sudhakar and Rohini, inviting them to join him on stage.

The unexpected gesture left Sudhakar visibly surprised. Nevertheless, he and Rohini walked toward the stage amidst applause. Vivek followed, presenting the couple with a flower bouquet and the gifts he had bought for them earlier. After receiving their blessings, Vivek stepped down from the stage.

Ashok continued, addressing the audience. "There's another story I would like to share. During one of my usual forest walks, a wild bear attacked me. I was caught off guard and unsure of what to do. A tribal man nearby rushed to my rescue, but he lost his hand in the process. His bravery left me deeply indebted. As a token of gratitude, I took on the responsibility of sponsoring his son's education and supporting their family. Today, that young man is pursuing a postgraduate degree in mass communication and journalism. I would like to invite them on stage."

At Ashok's invitation, Bago, the tribal man, and his son, Ramdas, joined him on stage. Ashok greeted them warmly and presented them with bouquets, expressing his heartfelt gratitude.

Concluding his presentation, Ashok reflected on his life experiences, including the loss of his wife, Sharadakka. He ended with a poignant line from Bhaja Govindam: "Punarapi Jananam, Punarapi Maranam" (Again birth, again death). The audience sat mesmerized, in awe of Ashok's humility and profound insights.

The next day, Sudhakar and his family prepared to return to Hubli. The thought of leaving left Sudhakar feeling heavy-hearted. His mind, however, was preoccupied with the revelations from the gathering.

For a moment, he thought he had finally unraveled the mystery behind Ashok's frequent visits to the house near Joida. But then, another realization struck him—there was no way the handsome young man he had seen during those visits was Bago's son. Sudhakar's thoughts spiraled. "Could this be the reason Ashok went into that house alone? Oh my God! Was Sharadakka betrayed, just as I feared?" His mind swirled with unanswered questions, leaving him deep in thought.

Sudhakar couldn't enjoy his dinner that night. Sensing this, Ashok decided it was time to reveal everything. He asked Sudhakar to sit with him on the slab in front of the house.

Ashok began, "Sudhakar, I have harbored this secret for decades. I think it's time I let it out. I know you've been suspicious of me, and I don't want anything to ruin our friendship. So, today, I will tell you everything.

The truth is, Ramdas is Kathyayini's son. Do you remember I told you about her relationship with Prof. Panchamukhi? Yes, Ramdas is their son. When we found out, I understood her decision to opt for an abortion. But by then, it was too late, and the process couldn't be carried out. Kathyayini had no choice but to keep the baby. She gave birth to him at Castlerock Hospital under Dr. Dinesh's care. He was a beautiful baby boy.

We couldn't keep the child, but abandoning him wasn't an option either. So, with a heavy heart, I gave the baby to Bago and his wife. The house I used to visit frequently was Bago's house. I would go there to check on Ramdas, play with him for a while, and support Bago and his family in any way I could. This is the truth behind my mysterious visits, Sudhakar."

Hearing this, Sudhakar was stunned. He sat there in silence, processing everything.

Ashok continued, his voice trembling, "I've grown weary of this Delhi life, my friend. Lately, I've been missing my mother more than ever. I curse myself for not taking better care of her. She was lonely, and I wasn't there for her when she needed me. She was a victim of time and circumstance, and I, her only son, failed her. I was a bad son, Sudhakar. I was a terrible son," Ashok confessed, tears streaming down his face. He broke down completely, sobbing uncontrollably.

Sudhakar didn't interrupt, knowing Ashok needed this moment to let out his long-held sorrow.

After some time, Ashok composed himself and shared his decision with Sudhakar. "I've decided to return to Sode and spend my remaining years in my mother's home. I'll take care of the Huliyappa and Maruti temples and devote the rest of my life to saving Mother Earth by working alongside Swarnavalli Swamiji."

Once Ashok had calmed down, Sudhakar gently held his hands and said, "Sir, I'm at a loss for words. I don't know what to say except this—you are extraordinary. You are a wonderful human being, and I am honored that you see my daughter as a suitable match for your son. I wholeheartedly agree to this alliance."

The two friends hugged each other tightly, their bond stronger than ever.

Sudhakar's mind felt clear, as bright as a sunny day. All his doubts and burdens vanished like clouds dissipating in the sky. That night, Sudhakar slept peacefully, his heart unburdened.

2

STRAWBERRY

"I wrote to her everyday for two years.
What do you think was the result?
She married the Postman"

-Leo Tolstoy

Arpita leaves her third-floor apartment in Chembur, West Mumbai, at exactly 9:30 a.m. every day. She is never a minute late. The faint scent of Chanel's Oakmoss fragrance lingers in the air as the impeccably dressed Arpita passes by the security room. She calls for an auto and waits in line across from Ratna Store. This routine unfolds like clockwork every single day.

Arpita works at a local bank, and there hasn't been a single day when she has failed to arrive on time. She is usually the third person to reach the bank, preceded only by the security guard Atmaram and the office attendant Shindhe. That particular day, before beginning her work, Arpita stepped into the break room and placed her lunchbox in the refrigerator. Her meal consisted of pulkas, sabzi, kakadi, curd, and a banana.

She made it a point to greet each of her colleagues with the sweetest smile and concluded her day with the same grace and enthusiasm.

As the youngest employee in the office, Arpita often found herself responsible for taking care of additional activities. Everyone's favorite manager, Deshmukh, was retiring soon, and her co-officer Gaitonde, who usually helped her, was unable to assist due to his ongoing struggle with asthma. This left Arpita to handle most of the bank's extra tasks. She was accustomed to managing everything so her colleagues could work seamlessly. Whenever the bank grew crowded, Arpita would rush to the counters to assist, ensuring smooth operations.

She had a particularly busy week ahead. Arpita, a management graduate from the Kousali Institute of Business Management, was known for her diligence and efficiency.

Her life, however, had not been without struggles. Arpita lost her mother, Shalini Taayi, at a young age, and her father died in a car crash. The only family she had left was her mausi, Jayashree. Yet, Arpita always carried herself with composure and grace, never letting her past define her.

That particular day, however, something felt off. Arpita appeared lost in her thoughts. When she returned home, she greeted her mausi and went straight to the washroom. Jayashree could hear faint sobs coming from inside, but she refrained from asking any questions.

When Arpita emerged, she had changed into fresh clothes and sat silently before the prayer room. She stared at the idols inside the mandir with a blank expression before closing her eyes. Jayashree watched as tears began to roll down Arpita's cheeks.

Concerned, Jayashree sat beside her and gently asked what was troubling her. Without saying a word, Arpita turned, hugged Jayashree tightly, and rested her head on her lap. Jayashree stroked her smooth hair gently, reassuring her that everything would be alright.

Jayashree assumed Arpita's tears were due to her worries about finding a life partner. Wiping the tears from the corners of Arpita's eyes, she said softly, "Everything is going to be alright, darling. Don't cry. You will find a good match soon. It's only a matter of time before your soulmate comes into your life. Everything will be alright, raja."

But Arpita was not crying about her wedding. In fact, marriage was the last thing on her mind. Whenever her mausi brought up the topic of marriage, Arpita would brush it aside and say, "Not right now. I still have plenty of time, and I'll let you know when I'm ready."

Jayashree, however, remained concerned about Arpita's wedding. Much like Arpita, Jayashree had faced her share of hardships in life. She had lost her husband at a young age, and her only son, a soldier stationed at the border, rarely called or visited. Arpita was the only person Jayashree could depend on, and to Jayashree, Arpita was more than a niece; she was like her own child.

At times, Jayashree would feel lonely and sit silently in a corner of the house, lost in thought. During such moments, Arpita would plan fun games to lift her spirits. Chess and card games were their favorites. Just as Arpita found ways to console her mausi, Jayashree would whip up Arpita's favorite dishes to cheer her up. The crispy pakoras paired with a cup of Wagh Bakri tea always brought a smile to Arpita's face, helping her forget her fatigue and sadness, if only for a while.

All Arpita truly desired in life was peace. She didn't care much about her outward appearance, but she never missed her daily workout routine. Unlike her colleagues, who dressed elaborately for work every day, Arpita kept her look simple. She avoided office gossip and minded her own business. While she respected everyone's individuality and their right to do what they felt was best, she was particular about one thing: her clothes. Arpita loved Fabindia in Lower Parel, and it was her go-to store. It was, in her words, her "happy place."

Arpita had been fiercely independent and responsible for her life choices since her college days. After earning a degree in science from St. Xavier's College in Mumbai, she decided to pursue an MSc from Karnataka University in Dharwad. This decision was entirely her own, despite her father's efforts to enroll her in a prestigious law school.

Arpita proved everyone wrong when she graduated with flying colors, even earning a gold medal. However, there was another reason for her decision to move to Dharwad. Around the same time, Jayashree's husband had passed away, leaving her to live alone. Although her son offered to help Jayashree relocate and live with him, she refused. She wanted to remain in Dharwad. Arpita moved to Dharwad not only for her education but also to support her mausi.

As mentioned earlier, Arpita had endured a lot before finding a stable job and building a comfortable life for herself and Jayashree. During a function organized for the gold medalists, Arpita addressed the crowd with humility. "I studied just like anyone else and earned a medal. There's nothing extraordinary about that. The real challenges and tasks lie ahead in life," she said. When asked if she had advice for young students, Arpita replied, "Let them study well. Knowledge is all we truly have." Even Dr. Subhash Chachadi, the Principal of the institute, described her as "an extraordinary girl."

Arpita soon secured a position in the national banking sector. Although the job required her to relocate to Mumbai, she accepted it without hesitation. She believed the move would be a positive change for both herself and her mausi. And just like that, Arpita became a part of India's largest city.

It so happened that Arpita's father owned a duplex house in South Mumbai. However, Arpita chose to find a place of her own. She had built her life independently so far without relying on her father's help, and she saw no reason to start now. She politely declined his offer of lodging. That didn't mean she cut ties with him; they continued to stay connected through phone calls every few days.

However, their conversations often became strained whenever the topic of marriage came up. Arpita's father would list out potential grooms, and Arpita, without fail, would find reasons to reject each one. At times, these discussions escalated into heated arguments, leaving her father frustrated and bewildered. In his eyes, Arpita, now 25, should have been married already. But no one took the time to understand why she was so opposed to the idea of marriage.

Arpita's aversion stemmed from an incident during her time in Dharwad. She had developed a deep admiration for a boy named Aravind Kulkarni, believing him to be her soulmate. They shared a close bond, often spending time at each other's homes. Arpita had even introduced him to her mausi, Jayashree, who liked him. On Fridays, the two would hold combined study sessions, alternating between their homes depending on the situation.

One such Friday, Aravind had relatives visiting his home, so he decided to come to Arpita's place for their session. Arpita agreed, as Jayashree was also going to be out that day. When Aravind arrived, she welcomed him as usual, offering cookies and juice before they began studying.

However, what started as an ordinary session quickly turned into a nightmare. Without warning, Aravind grabbed Arpita, forcefully kissed her, and groped her while pushing her against the wall. Arpita was momentarily paralyzed by shock but soon regained her composure. Furious, she slapped him hard across the face, cursed him, and threw him out of the house.

The incident left a deep scar on Arpita. She felt betrayed and lost all trust in men. From that day on, she kept her distance from the entire male gender, refusing to let anyone get too close.

Even after moving to Mumbai, Arpita encountered similar challenges. At her workplace, there was an old Brigadier who would frequently stare at her with unsettling intent. Initially, she ignored his behavior, hoping he would stop. But when his actions persisted, Arpita reached her limit and decided to confront him.

"Excuse me," she said firmly. "Why do you keep staring at me? I've made it clear that your behavior makes me uncomfortable, yet you refuse to stop. If this continues, I will have no choice but to report you."

Her words left the Brigadier visibly startled, but Arpita remained unshaken. She had learned to stand her ground, refusing to tolerate disrespect from anyone.

The Brigadier, instead of apologizing, replied that Arpita seemed like a good match for his son, who was a dentist. He made no effort to acknowledge how uncomfortable he had made her feel.

"You don't see the need to apologize to me?" Arpita asked curtly. "Anyway, stop staring at me. And please refrain from discussing personal matters during bank hours." With that, she walked away, leaving the Brigadier visibly taken aback.

For Arpita, life was the greatest teacher. She had little regard for management books written by celebrated scholars, dismissing them as impractical. In her view, they were useless in real-life situations. Arpita believed in learning through practical experiences. To her, Mumbai itself was the ultimate management guru. She had utter disdain for terms like "management guru," "health guru," or "relationship guru," often calling them "nonsense." She regarded these labels and techniques as mere money-making schemes.

If anyone tried to challenge her views, Arpita would counter with her trademark question: "Okay, so tell me, how did our local dabbawalas or the orphan kids and illiterates working at Lijjat Papad learn management? Did they become experts by reading your thick books, or did they learn through real-life experiences?"

Arpita often found solace in the discourses of Guru Samarth Ramdas or the soulful Marathi Abhangs sung by Kishori Amonkar. When she felt particularly melancholic, Ghulam Ali's ghazals were her refuge. At other times, she enjoyed listening to Guru Gopal Das, appreciating his light-hearted jokes and simple sermons.

Though she preferred solitude, Arpita occasionally attended her colleagues' family functions. She also spent time with Apte, an elderly man who lived in the same apartment building. Apte, a retired banker, had a son and daughter-in-law who lived in Dubai. He visited them every year, only to return after falling out with them.

Despite being 70, Apte's youthful energy was infectious. One of his favorite songs to sing was "Khushi Raho, Yeh Khushi Hai Tumhare Liye..." by Khushwant Singh, which he would hum with great enthusiasm.

Arpita had hired a maid, Kamala Ben, to help with household chores, as she didn't want her mausi to take on extra work. Over time, Kamala had become more like a family member. She took care of Arpita with the affection of a sister.

On weekends, Kamala would oil Arpita's hair, wash it with warm water, and dry it with loban. While massaging Arpita's head, Kamala would often muse, "I wonder where your prince charming is. I'm sure he's waiting for you." Though Arpita didn't appreciate such comments, she never voiced her disapproval. Instead, she would smile politely and turn away.

After a long, relaxing bath, Kamala would serve Arpita a meal of hot methi thepla, coconut chutney, rice, dal, and dahi. This weekend routine became a source of comfort for Arpita, leaving her feeling rejuvenated and helping her sleep peacefully at night.

Arpita's father, Purushottam Jog, was a renowned legal practitioner at the Bombay High Court. He had amassed significant wealth through his career. If Arpita wished, she could have chosen to live comfortably off her father's fortune without working.

Mr. Jog had completed his legal education at the Government Law College in Mumbai and established his own successful private practice. With his well-built physique, commanding voice, and exceptional oratory skills, he seemed tailor-made for his profession. He was widely respected for his flawless legal opinions and unparalleled expertise.

One of Mr. Jog's most notable achievements was restoring property worth crores of rupees belonging to the Peshwas, which had been wrongfully acquired by the Government. This legal victory, achieved after a fierce courtroom battle, earned him immense admiration. As a gesture of gratitude, the Peshwas gifted him six acres of fertile land and a well-furnished bungalow in Mahabaleshwar.

Purushottam hailed from a joint family in Kelshi, a village located in the Konkan strip of Ratnagiri district. His ancestral bungalow, nestled amidst areca and coconut trees, was set against a breathtaking natural backdrop. Occasionally, he would visit this family home with his wife, Shalini, and daughter, Arpita, traveling in his Ambassador car. Known as "Kaka" within the family, he delighted in the delicious mangoes grown in their garden. These visits were etched in his memory, and even years later, he would fondly share these stories with Arpita.

However, Mr. Jog's happiness was short-lived. One evening, while preparing dinner, Shalini suddenly collapsed. Purushottam rushed her to Jaslok Hospital, where doctors worked tirelessly through the night but ultimately could do nothing. The attending physician approached Mr. Jog with a heavy heart and said, "Vakil Saheb, I regret to inform you that Shalini has an irrecoverable nerve disease. She will likely remain bedridden for the rest of her life. I suggest you take her home and arrange for care."

Purushottam was devastated by the news. He sank to the floor, overwhelmed with grief, and sat motionless for several minutes. But he soon realized that Shalini needed him now more than ever, and he resolved to be her pillar of strength.

Following the doctor's advice, he brought Shalini home and hired a house nurse to provide round-the-clock care. Recognizing the challenges of raising young Arpita while managing his career and caring for Shalini, he also employed a tutor to help Arpita with her schoolwork.

In a difficult decision, Purushottam sold the ancestral house in Kelshi to an industrialist for a significant sum. With this money, he purchased a duplex house on Pedder Road in Mumbai, intending to build a stable future for his family.

Despite his unwavering efforts, no medicine on earth could cure Shalini's rare condition. After enduring years of pain, Shalini passed away, finally finding peace.

Shalini's death was a crushing blow to Mr. Jog. He struggled to come to terms with her absence and found it impossible to fill the void she had left in his life. His worries now extended to Arpita, who was entering her formative years without a mother's guidance. The burden of raising her and providing her with emotional support weighed heavily on him.

When Arpita left for Dharwad for her higher studies, accompanied by her widowed aunt, Mr. Jog was left all alone in his expansive house. It was during this period that a new person entered his life—Payal Mistry. Payal had been working as an assistant in Mr. Jog's law firm for over 15 years and was five years younger than him.

One day, Payal approached Mr. Jog and candidly expressed her wish to cohabitate with him. She explained that she, too, was lonely, having been divorced for five years. While Mr. Jog didn't respond immediately, he seriously considered Payal's proposal. Payal was a mother of two, and Mr. Jog thought she could be a good companion, someone who might help him overcome his solitude.

Eventually, Mr. Jog decided to accept Payal's suggestion. However, he didn't consult his daughter, sister-in-law, or any other family members before embarking on this new chapter of his life. He braced himself for resistance from Arpita, as he thought it would be a natural reaction. To his surprise, Arpita understood his situation with remarkable maturity.

"Kaka," she said, "please forgive me. I never thought about how lonely you might feel. If living with Payal brings you happiness, please go ahead."

Purushottam felt relieved and grateful for his daughter's understanding. Arpita also made an effort to get to know Payal and even tried to find traces of her lost mother in her. The three often went out for dinner together, and Arpita grew fond of Payal's carrot halwa, always asking for an extra serving. For a while, things were peaceful, and everyone seemed happy.

However, this idyllic picture didn't last long.

While returning from a holiday at the Khandala resort, Purushottam and Payal met with a fatal accident. Both died on the spot. Their bodies were so severely mangled that they were barely recognizable. The names Purushottam Jog and Payal Mistry, once prominent in Mumbai's legal world, were now consigned to history.

Arpita was devastated. It felt as though life kept testing her resilience with one tragedy after another. Despite her grief, she managed to pull herself together to perform her father's last rites. She spread his ashes in the Godavari River at Trayambak, fulfilling his final rites with a heavy heart.

Although Arpita hadn't met her father every day, she had always found comfort in knowing he was there for her, someone she could turn to if she ever needed support. His sudden death left a void in her life. Yet, over time, she found healing and learned to live a contented life with her mausi, Jayashree. While the memories of her tragic past would sometimes bring her to tears, Arpita had largely made peace with her life.

The next day, as part of her usual routine, Arpita left her house and waited for an auto. On her way to the bank, her eyes fell on a basket of fresh strawberries by the roadside. A smart young man sat on a stool, selling the fruit. Arpita was instantly drawn to the sight— not just because of the man's charm but also because of her love for strawberries.

As a child, Arpita had fond memories of eating juicy strawberries during trips to Mahabaleshwar with her father. The sight of the strawberries brought those cherished moments flooding back, momentarily taking her mind off her present life.

Arpita stopped the auto abruptly and hurried toward the young man selling strawberries. She quickly began picking some, and the young man assisted her in selecting the tastiest ones.

"How much do you want, madam?" he asked.

"Half a kilogram, please," Arpita replied, raising her eyebrows slightly.

As she handed him the money, Arpita found herself observing how attractive and humble the young man was. Her heart raced, and she couldn't ignore the butterflies in her stomach. With the bag of strawberries in hand, she caught another auto and headed to her office.

The very next day, Arpita found herself stopping by his stall again, purchasing another half kilogram of strawberries.

Surprised, the young man asked, "Madam, you just bought strawberries yesterday, and you're back for another half kilo today. May I ask how many members live in your house?" His question came in the local Mumbai Hindi dialect.

Arpita paused, realizing he had a point. "Why am I here again?" she wondered to herself. She smiled awkwardly, paid for the strawberries, and left without a word.

After that day, it became a routine. Each morning, on her way to work, Arpita would glance at the young man and smile. On days when he wasn't there, her eyes would instinctively search for him. It wasn't a one-sided affair; the young man also began waiting for her to pass by every day.

As time passed, they started chatting, and a strong friendship blossomed. The young man revealed only that he was the son of a teacher from Ayodhya but said little else about his life. Arpita, too, shared minimal details, simply introducing herself as a bank employee at a nearby branch.

Despite the limited exchange of personal information, their connection deepened, with strawberries remaining the thread that tied them together.

One day, unable to suppress her feelings any longer, Arpita blurted out, "I like you."

The young man was stunned into silence, and before he could respond, Arpita rushed away, her face flushed with embarrassment.

That night, Arpita tossed and turned, unable to sleep. "Did I rush into this? Should I have waited?" she wondered, her thoughts swirling. Memories of her speech at the Kousali Institute's valedictory function resurfaced: "My future is my achievement," she had declared with confidence.

Now, lying in bed, she chuckled to herself. "I've fallen in love with a strawberry seller. Is this my grand achievement?" she mused. As she stared at the ceiling, the image of a red strawberry and a green cap danced before her eyes. Her thoughts drifted to the tragic love story of Mera Naam Joker. Tears welled up, and she wept silently, letting all her emotions pour out.

The next morning, she woke up with a bright smile, hugged her aunt tightly, and exclaimed, "Aunty, I got the boy!"

Jayashree, utterly confused, asked, "Arpita! What are you talking about? Can you please explain? I don't understand a thing!"

But Arpita danced around the room, grinning from ear to ear, and replied cryptically, "What's next is a secret!" She left for work without offering any further explanation.

The following day, Arpita visited the strawberry stall again. As she picked out a few strawberries, she looked directly at the young man and said, "Look, I've decided. I have feelings for you, and I think you're the one for me. If I'm ever going to marry, it'll be you and only you."

Her words spilled out without hesitation, leaving the young man visibly stunned.

The young man lost his composure. Standing up abruptly from his chair, he exclaimed, "Excuse me? Do you even realize what you're saying? Does this all look like a joke to you? Do you think marriage is a child's game?"

"No, it's not a joke. I know exactly what I'm asking," Arpita replied, her voice trembling. "Believe me, I thought about it all night. I didn't even want to get married, ever. But there's something about you—some connection. If I am to marry in this life, it has to be you. Next week, let's visit your father in Ayodhya and tell him about us," she said, breathless but resolute.

Without waiting for a response, Arpita turned and rushed to an auto, disappearing toward her bank.

On her way to work, Arpita's phone rang. It was her late father's assistant. "Beti," the voice began, "I'm calling to inform you about your late father's will. Purushottam delegated all his properties to your name. And there's another thing—Payal has nominated her house at Malabar Hill not in your name, but in the name of the child you will have one day."

Arpita, caught off guard, responded, "Let us discuss this later…." The call left her confused and deep in thought as she headed to the bank.

A week passed in the blink of an eye. True to their plan, Arpita and the young man, Alok, reached Ayodhya late one evening. Alok led her to his family home—a modest, well-kept house, the third one on the lane, named Tripathi. The house, though rented, had a welcoming charm. Alok's parents were its sole occupants, as his sister was married and Alok lived away for work.

Alok's parents were visibly shocked when their son arrived unannounced—and even more so when they saw him accompanied by a young woman. Before formalities could begin, Arpita stepped forward and introduced herself. She then confidently explained her feelings for Alok and their decision to get married.

To her relief, Alok's parents were happy. They had no reason to oppose the match and welcomed the couple inside. As they all sat together, enjoying tea and snacks, Alok's father broke the silence.

"Beti," he said, addressing Arpita, "do you think a marriage between a banker and an engineer will be a good match?"

Arpita froze, shocked. Engineer? She had no idea about this side of Alok.

Sensing her surprise, Alok stepped in to clarify. "I should have told you sooner," he began, turning to Arpita.

Alok explained that he had graduated from IIT Kharagpur and worked as an engineer in Delhi. However, he had to quit when he discovered that the company's chief was misusing his technical expertise for unethical purposes. Disillusioned, he took a train and ended up in Mumbai without a clear plan.

On the train, Alok met Bhairu, a fruit vendor, and decided to assist him with his sales to make ends meet. Meanwhile, he had secured a job training a US-based student in Salesforce management, earning a decent salary of ₹50,000 per month.

Since this job required only three hours of work each night, Alok spent his days selling strawberries alongside Bhairu. It was during these hours that he and Arpita had crossed paths.

As Alok finished his explanation, Arpita felt a mix of emotions—shock, admiration, and relief. This man, who had faced setbacks yet carved his own path, was unlike anyone she had ever met.

Arpita was taken aback by Alok's revelation. She stared at him in silence for a moment, and then both of them broke into laughter. It was a moment of shared relief and joy, as though the honesty had brought them even closer.

They relished the samosas and tea lovingly served by Alok's mother, chatting like long-lost friends. The conversation flowed naturally, filled with stories, laughter, and a sense of familiarity.

After a while, like any typical Indian father, Tripathi cleared his throat and said, "Dear daughter, there's something you should know. We live in a rented house. I have no property or significant savings. We are not very well-off."

Arpita smiled warmly, her face radiating sincerity. "Uncle, you don't have to worry about any of that. Alok is my treasure. I don't need anything else. Let's all move to Mahabaleshwar and settle there. I've just inherited a house in that beautiful place."

Tripathi was taken aback by her generosity, but he could see the honesty in her eyes. The family continued to talk, savoring the simplicity of the moment.

They spent the entire night chatting, and before they realized it, the first rays of dawn had begun to creep in. Alok's parents decided to step out to buy fresh groceries, planning to cook a hearty meal for Alok and Arpita.

As soon as the parents left, Arpita turned to Alok, her eyes sparkling with mischief. She hugged him tightly and said, "You cheat. You've stolen my heart all over again."

Alok chuckled, holding her close. They kissed, the affection and connection between them deepening with each moment. In that embrace, they drifted into their own world, a space where time seemed to pause, and only their love existed.

3

DISPOSITION

Surprisingly, Appanna Bhat had returned home much earlier than expected that day after performing the Ekadasha Rudra at Subray Hegde's residence. Normally, it would be quite late by the time Appanna reached home, as his priestly duties often stretched well into the evening at the houses of his disciples. His routine usually included a heavy lunch at his host's house, followed by a short nap, a cup of evening tea, and then a ride home on one of his students' scooters.

But that day was different. He had come home early.

Sharadakka, his wife, was pleasantly surprised to see him at such an hour. However, Appanna's demeanor was unusual—he wasn't his usual calm and composed self. He hurried inside, removing his footwear, and asked anxiously, "Has anybody come home?"

After quickly washing his hands and feet, Appanna freshened up and sat in his usual spot. Sharadakka offered him a cup of fresh buttermilk to quench his thirst. Despite the refreshment, his face looked sunken, and the dullness in his dark brown complexion was unmistakable. Appanna seemed distant, lost in thoughts that Sharadakka could only guess at. He silently drank the buttermilk without a word.

For the past week, Appanna had been far from his usual cheerful self. He seemed preoccupied, burdened by something only he knew. Sharadakka was deeply concerned; he had never been one to share his worries or troubles with her.

Breaking the silence, Sharadakka hesitated before speaking. "So, Salakodu Shivaram came home about two hours ago," she began. "He brought an elderly couple with him. They went around the house, inspected the cattle shed, and even checked the well. I couldn't make out what they were saying, but they were murmuring among themselves. The couple didn't look like they were from around here. And they weren't here to show their horoscopes—they barely spoke to me but seemed to be carefully inspecting every corner of the house. I'm completely puzzled. I don't know what they were up to!"

Appanna listened without showing much reaction, as if he had anticipated this. He didn't seem surprised. Instead, he simply nodded in acknowledgment, saying nothing. He stood up after a while and began walking around the house, examining it silently. He stayed outside until darkness began to settle.

As night fell, Appanna washed his hands and feet again and entered the pooja room. Sitting cross-legged before the Lord, he began chanting the Sri Sthuti with intense focus. Appanna was deeply devoted, and once he entered the pooja room, nothing could distract him.

That evening, Appanna slid into deep meditation, completely immersed in prayer. While he was in this state, he seemed to hear the voice of his late father, Shambu Bhattaru, as clearly as if he were right there.

"Appanna," the voice said, "sit before the Lord whenever you are in trouble and surrender yourself to Him. It's okay to cry in front of the Lord. Speak to Him, say everything that burdens your heart. Pray with utmost devotion, and He will show you the path."

Appanna's mind was overwhelmed with memories of his late parents. They had tragically lost their lives during a pilgrimage to Kedarnath, swept away in the devastating flood caused by a sudden cloudburst. The disaster claimed countless innocent lives. In an instant, Appanna lost a piece of himself. His father's long-held wish to perform the Sahasra Chandra Darshan upon their return from the pilgrimage remained unfulfilled, leaving Appanna with a deep sense of incompleteness.

He couldn't stop thinking about the happy times when his parents were alive, standing by his side. His father's wisdom and guidance, paired with his mother's unconditional love, had made him feel whole. And yet, in a single moment, that completeness vanished, leaving him with an emptiness he couldn't shake.

After a few more minutes of reminiscing, Appanna came back to his senses. His thoughts shifted to the news his son, Narasimha, had shared with him over the phone. Narasimha, who had settled in Bengaluru as a software engineer, had recently called. Appanna was happy to hear from his son initially, but the conversation left him shaken. The shocking reason behind Narasimha's call rendered Appanna speechless for several moments before he could muster a response.

As if that wasn't enough, Appanna's nephew and student, Venkati, added to his turmoil on his way home that day. "Uncle, have you heard the rumors spreading about your daughter Girija?" Venkati began. "The whole village is saying she's been having an affair with the cook, Nagesh. You need to act quickly, Uncle, or it could ruin her reputation. What if this affects her chances of getting marriage proposals?"

Appanna felt his heart sink. He didn't have the strength to process these two pieces of unsettling news. He was at a complete loss, unsure where to begin or how to react.

Appanna had three children. His eldest daughter, Nagaveni, was married to Sridhar, Appanna's sister's son, and lived in Neelakodu.

His only son, Narasimha, was a software engineer settled in Bengaluru. His youngest, Girija, had completed her BA and was yet to be married.

Girija was an intelligent and active young woman with a strong sense of purpose. She was involved in various gramapanchayat activities, working for the betterment of women in the village. She often spoke passionately about independence and ethical living, earning admiration from many in the community.

However, Appanna had also heard whispers about Girija spending time with Nagesh, a caterer from their village. Nagesh, whom Appanna had watched grow up, had completed his education and returned to the village to pursue his passion for cooking. He was known to be an honest and hardworking young man.

Just two days ago, Nagesh's father had visited Appanna. He seemed hesitant, fumbling with his words before finally revealing the purpose of his visit. He wanted to show Appanna Nagesh's horoscope. But as Appanna was in a hurry, Nagesh's father left the horoscope on the table, saying he would return later.

Now, with all these thoughts swirling in his mind, Appanna felt drained and distracted. He had lost his focus. Rising from the floor of the pooja room, he folded his hands, bowed his head before the Lord, and walked out.

* * *

It was past nine o'clock at night when Narasimha boarded a bus leaving from Jayanagar Fourth Block in Bengaluru, heading towards Honnavar. He seemed lost in his thoughts.

He stretched out on his seat, his mind preoccupied. Earlier that evening, he had hurried home from the office, quickly packing a few clothes into a bag—whatever he could find. He gulped down the upma his wife, Lalitha, had prepared, along with a cup of milk, and then left home in a rush. Taking an autorickshaw to the bus stop, he had barely paused to catch his breath.

Narasimha usually felt a wave of joy whenever he visited his hometown. The thought of meeting his parents always excited him. But this time was different. This time, he was anxious, unsure of how his father would react to the proposal he carried. The uncertainty weighed heavily on him, and he couldn't sleep a wink on the bus.

For the past eight years, Narasimha had been living in Bengaluru with his wife, Lalitha, and their daughter, Sadhvi, in a rented house. Like any family, Narasimha and Lalitha dreamt of owning a home and providing the best education for their daughter. After considerable effort, Narasimha had managed to secure Sadhvi's admission to Kumaran School for nursery.

To make this possible, they had rented a house in Banashankari, even though it meant enduring long commutes to and from Narasimha's office. Every day, as he passed by the under-construction Mantri apartment complex, Narasimha would imagine owning a flat there—a home of his own in the city.

But dreams came with a price. Narasimha had little savings in his bank account, and the thought of buying a house seemed daunting. It would require a significant amount of money—money he didn't have.

Lalitha, however, had a suggestion. "What if we sell your ancestral property in your parents' village? We could get your parents to move to Bengaluru and stay with us," she proposed.

Her plan had multiple advantages. With Narasimha's parents living with them, Lalitha could finally focus on finishing her beautician course and landing a job—aspirations she had put on hold to care for their young daughter. Having her in-laws at home would mean she could count on them to help with Sadhvi and the household chores.

But Narasimha wasn't entirely convinced. He knew his parents' deep emotional connection to their ancestral home. That house and the village were not just pieces of land to them—they were filled with memories and a sense of belonging. Moving them to Bengaluru, away from the familiarity and comfort of their roots, felt like asking too much. Forcing them to adapt to an entirely new environment at their age didn't sit well with him.

Narasimha's thoughts drifted to a memory of how devastated his father, Appanna, had been when they had to uproot a coconut tree in front of their ancestral house. His parents had always been deeply attached to the home—it wasn't just a structure but a treasure trove of memories and emotions.

From the very beginning, Narasimha was against Lalitha's idea of selling the ancestral property. He empathized with his parents' connection to the house and knew that the proposal would deeply hurt them. However, Lalitha, self-centered as she could be, had the upper hand in their discussions. Their disagreements often escalated into heated arguments, and eventually, Lalitha managed to convince Narasimha to at least present the idea to his father.

In preparation, Narasimha had already reached out to one of his friends, Shivaram, and asked him to scout for suitable buyers. Shivaram found an interested buyer, but there was one complication—they were not of the same caste.

When Shivaram informed Appanna about the potential buyer, Appanna, feeling cornered and helpless, had requested Narasimha to come home so they could discuss the matter in person.

The bus came to a halt in Shivamogga for a break. Narasimha got off, bought a tender coconut to quench his thirst, and returned to his seat. As the bus resumed its journey, exhaustion finally took over, and Narasimha drifted into a restless sleep.

* * *

That day was unlike any other for Appanna. He had completed his morning bath and pooja rituals well before 8:00 a.m. and mentally prepared himself for the important conversation he was about to have with his son. Appanna had requested his eldest daughter, Nagaveni, and her husband, Sridhar, to visit him as he wanted them to be present during the discussion. The couple had arrived from Neelakodu the previous night.

Appanna sat cross-legged on the Krishnajina—a deer skin spread over a wooden plank. His forehead bore the sacred Vibuthi, giving him the appearance of a dignified saint. Around his neck, he wore a string of Rudraksha beads, and his bright eyes reflected both wisdom and resolve. Appanna had also asked Sharadakka, his wife, to join the meeting. The small gathering included his son-in-law Sridhar, daughter Nagaveni, Nagesh, and Nagesh's father, Subbanna. They were all seated, waiting for Narasimha's arrival.

Within minutes, Narasimha arrived, freshened up, and joined the gathering. Without further delay, the discussion began.

Appanna started, his voice calm but commanding. "Thank you all for accepting my request and being here on such short notice. I have two important matters to discuss today."

He paused briefly before continuing, ensuring everyone was attentive. "My son Narasimha has proposed that we sell this ancestral house and move to Bengaluru to stay with him and his family. He suggests we sell this house to people we do not even know. Let me tell you this—this house was built by my ancestors, and generations of our family have lived happily under this roof. This land has given me everything. I have neighbors here whom I can trust with my life. If I were ever in need, one word from me and they would be here to help. This house and this land represent tradition, stability, and blessings from our family deity, who has always guided us. I cannot abandon this place."

He paused again, his gaze moving across the room to ensure his words were being understood. "Narasimha, I know you mean well and want to take care of your mother and me in our old age. I appreciate that. But I have seen too many parents regret leaving their homes and moving to distant places. My wife and I will live here for the rest of our lives. There will be no further discussion on this matter. We are not moving."

Appanna's voice grew firmer. "However," he continued, "I have saved some money over the years. I can give that money to Narasimha to help him buy a house in Bengaluru. In addition, I have decided to divide my wealth equally among my children. But…" He stopped mid-sentence, his gaze fixed on Narasimha.

"But Narasimha," he resumed, "you must give Girija her rightful share of the inheritance. This is a condition, and it is non-negotiable."

He turned his attention to Girija and Nagesh. "Girija," he said gently, "I have heard that you have developed a liking for Nagesh. I am also aware of the rumors circulating in the village about you both. If you believe Nagesh is the right match for you, you have my blessings to proceed with this relationship. I have examined both of your horoscopes, and they align well. You can stay here in this house and continue with your respective businesses. Your presence here will also be helpful for your mother and me as we grow older. This is my decision."

With these words, Appanna stood up and walked into the house. The meeting was concluded.

Shortly afterward, the sound of the bell from the pooja room echoed through the house—a symbol of Appanna's contentment and clarity of purpose.

4

INAS MAMA AND HIS POSTBAG

"I always like walking in the rain, so no one can see me crying."
– Charlie Chaplin

"Where does Inas mama live?"

Ask anyone in Toppalakeri, and they will immediately point you to a tiny, weathered house just a few kilometers away from the Arabian Sea. Nestled near NH 66, this quaint village lies between Honnavar and Kumta, two prominent towns in the Uttara Kannada district. Toppalakeri is a harmonious blend of people from diverse communities and religions. But if you think knowing the location of Inas mama's house guarantees you'll find him there, you're mistaken.

Don't picture Inas mama as a man swamped with responsibilities or running errands all day. His life has a steady rhythm, punctuated by simple routines.

Here's what his day typically looks like: Inas wakes up early and takes charge of all the household chores at his daughter Mary's house. He prepares breakfast while simultaneously working on lunch. Once the food is ready, he helps his young granddaughter get dressed for school, packs her lunch bag, and ensures everything is in place. Finally, he escorts both his daughter and granddaughter to the Honnavar bus stop and bids them farewell as they board the bus.

Once his family is off for the day, Inas returns home to an empty house. His solitary hours are spent in a humble routine—sitting on a wooden bench with yarn, dried leaves, and tobacco chips, skillfully rolling beedis. These beedis are highly sought after in the village and can only be found at Lakkanna's tea shop.

Whenever monotony sets in, Inas heads to the Sarpakarneshwar River with his fishing line in hand. He meditates on the stone footbridge spanning the stream, waiting patiently for a tug on the line. As he sits there, his mind drifts into memories, reliving the ups and downs of his life.

Inas often thinks of his late wife, Abrooze, who left him too soon. They had shared a happy life until financial hardships disrupted their peace. His mind frequently returns to the pain of his daughter's failed marriage. He had married her off to his nephew, hoping the union would shield her from life's hardships. But his trust was betrayed—his nephew not only demanded money but also physically abused her. The marriage eventually fell apart.

Adding to his woes was his grown son, Victor, who, at 25, remained unemployed and completely dependent on Inas. Victor showed no inclination to stand on his own feet and often created trouble for his sister, demanding money from her.

Haunted by these worries, Inas's fishing meditation often ended in tears. With his heart heavy, he would pray aloud to Jesus, questioning his misfortunes. "Oh Lord, what sins have I committed in my previous life? Why do You burden me with so much pain? Where did I go wrong?"

But eventually, a tug on the fishing line would break his lamentations, bringing him back to the present. After catching enough fish, Inas would head home with a slightly lighter heart, ready to face another day.

No one had ever seen Inas cry. His tears were reserved for the solitude of the stream, where he could freely let out his sorrows. Around his friends and family, Inas wore a mask of happiness, hiding his inner turmoil behind a warm smile. He kept his pain locked away, even from his daughter and granddaughter, never allowing them to see his unhappiness.

Every evening, after his granddaughter returned from school, Inas spent over an hour with her. Her friends would often join them because Inas had a gift for storytelling. He regaled the children with tales of princesses trapped in towering forts by evil demons and other captivating stories, each with a valuable moral. At the end of these sessions, he handed out sweets he had purchased with his earnings from selling beedis.

Being surrounded by children brought Inas a sense of peace and purpose. On days when his fishing was fruitful, he shared his catch with his neighbors. Helping others became his solace, and he never hesitated when someone needed assistance. Whether it was rushing a sick neighbor to the hospital or helping decorate homes during Christmas, Inas was always there. Over time, he earned the affectionate title of "Inas mama," becoming a beloved figure in the village. People sought him out whenever they faced problems, trusting his wisdom and kind heart.

Though Inas made a living rolling beedis, he was never seen smoking or loitering in tea shops like other villagers. He led his life guided by simple principles—content, modest, and free from complaints or demands.

But life has a way of testing even the kindest souls. One day, the government announced plans to widen the National Highway, which meant demolishing houses along the road. Despite protests and appeals, Inas's ancestral home, a place where generations of his family had lived and died, was torn down. The loss left him and his family homeless, both physically and emotionally shattered.

The government offered compensation, but the money barely covered their expenses. Inas's daughter deposited what little they had into a bank account, which was enough to provide for their basic needs. But their most pressing need—a roof over their heads—remained unmet.

Help came from an unexpected source. John, a forest official with a kind heart, stepped in to save the day. John owned a beautiful ancestral property in Honnavar, and he offered it to Inas. "Mama," he said, "I know what you're going through. You need a place to call home. Here are the keys to my property. Stay there rent-free for as long as you need."

Overwhelmed by John's generosity, Inas's eyes filled with tears. "May Jesus bless you, John! May the Lord bless you!" he cried, hugging John tightly and expressing his heartfelt gratitude.

Moving into John's house brought stability back into Inas's life. Not a single day passed without Inas praying for John and his kindness. However, John was not a stranger to Inas. He had known John since childhood and watched him grow into a kind young man. In fact, John and Inas's daughter had grown up together and had once shared feelings for each other. But Inas had rejected John's proposal, favoring his nephew, who seemed more stable and well-settled in Mumbai.

If only Inas could have foreseen the future, his daughter might have married John and lived a life filled with love and happiness.

Inas might have chosen his nephew over John because he believed his nephew's stable income in Mumbai would ensure a comfortable life for his daughter. However, destiny had other plans. The nephew, as it turned out, had lied about his circumstances. He indulged in drinking, smoking, and other vices, neglecting Mary completely. Even after Mary gave birth to their daughter, he viewed them as burdens and eventually sent them back to Inas's house.

Moving into John's house provided a roof over their heads, but life was far from easy for Inas and his family. They barely managed to get through each month. Once a week, the family would attend church. Whenever he went to church, Inas wore an age-old coat tailored by his father, Antony. Though the coat was worn and out of fashion, it served the practical purpose of covering the torn shirt Inas wore underneath.

That coat often transported Inas down memory lane. His father, Antony, was a professional tailor, though he had struggled with stitching coats. Yet Antony had been determined to make a coat for Inas, working painstakingly through more than ten fittings before it finally fit perfectly. He had dreamed of seeing Inas wear the coat on his wedding day. When the coat was finally complete, the joy on Antony's face was indescribable. Inas couldn't help but smile as he relived those precious memories.

Inas loved going to church, not just for the solace it offered but also for the companionship of Father Francis Lobo. Known as the "Father of Love," Father Lobo was beloved in the town for his teachings on love and humanity. He often quoted St. Paul, emphasizing that without love—love for humanity and love for others—one was nothing. Father Lobo frequently joked, "Learn to smile like our Inas here." Embarrassed by the attention, Inas would laugh nervously and reply, "Father is just joking," while shrugging it off.

Father Lobo was more than just a spiritual guide; he was a lifeline for Inas's family. He had helped Mary secure a job at St. Joseph's School and shared a deep, mutual respect with Inas. Yet, despite the support, Inas remained troubled by his son Victor's behavior. Victor often disappeared for days at a time and, when he was home, would lock himself in his room, speaking to no one. He appeared depressed and lost. Deeply concerned, Inas confided in Father Lobo, who managed to get Victor admitted to a diploma course. But even this didn't fully ease Inas's worries.

Time passed, and life carried on. Inas mama was not one to sit idly or rely on others. He was always active, refusing to eat food he hadn't earned. On some days, Inas would work late into the evening at the church, finding satisfaction in being productive. He felt immense joy whenever Father Lobo handed him some food with fish curry after a long day. True to his selfless nature, Inas would always bring a portion of that food back home to share with his daughter and granddaughter.

We have seen enough of Inas's tragic life. Let me now share a glimpse of his happier days. Karki was a small village, not densely populated but still bustling with life. The village had schools, temples, ration stores, laundry services, and other basic amenities.

The village boasted two talented tailors—Antony, Inas's father, and another man named Bikka. Antony's shop was located next to Upendra Pai's grocery shop, while Bikka's shop was beside Vithal Bhandarkar's grocery store. Antony was known for his expertise in stitching men's wear, such as pyjamas, shirts, underwear, and baniyans (vests). On the other hand, Bikka specialized in women's clothing. Antony had a loyal customer base who greatly appreciated his craftsmanship. His baniyans, in particular, were in high demand not only in Karki but also in neighboring towns. Renowned locals like Chandra Master and Gundu Master were regular patrons of Antony's shop.

There were times when Antony struggled to meet deadlines due to overwhelming orders. During such times, he would ask his son, Inas, to lend a hand. Antony was not only talented but also widely respected for his dedication and skill. Antony had a dream for his son. Since Inas wasn't excelling academically, Antony hoped his son would take up tailoring and carry forward his legacy. To that end, Antony sent Inas to Kumta to train under the guidance of tailor Venkatesh. Unfortunately, despite Antony's efforts, Inas struggled to grasp the trade. Realizing that tailoring wasn't his son's forte, Antony called Inas back home and had him sit by his side in the shop, observing and assisting where he could.

One day, Rukkayya Shanubhog, a prominent figure in Karki, visited Antony's tailoring shop. Antony was pleasantly surprised to see him. Rukkayya had come to get a white kurta stitched for his daughter's wedding. As he conversed with Antony, his eyes fell on Inas, who was seated nearby. Rukkayya noted Inas's youthful charm and couldn't help but smile. As he observed Inas, an idea began forming in his mind. "I think Inas might be the solution to the problem that's been troubling me for a week," Rukkayya thought to himself with a knowing smile.

Rukkayya had recently identified a lucrative opportunity in extracting oil from honne seeds, which were commonly used as grease for wheels and fishing boats. He envisioned setting up an oil mill in Karki to capitalize on this business idea. Seeing Inas, he believed the young man would be the perfect fit to help him run the mill. Ishwar, the son of Narayan and a supplier of fish to Rukkayya, was another contender for the role, but Rukkayya saw something special in Inas.

After discussing the details of his kurta order with Antony, Rukkayya broached the subject of his business idea. "Antony, I've been working on a plan for a new business, and I think your son Inas could be an excellent fit for it," Rukkayya said, his tone full of optimism. "May I take him with me now to see if he'd be suitable for the role?" he asked, seeking Antony's permission.

Antony was elated by Rukkayya's proposal. He had been contemplating ways to help Inas secure a stable job, and this opportunity seemed perfect. Without hesitation, Antony gave his approval and sent Inas along with Rukkayya.

The oil mill was established in Karki in no time. Under the diligent oversight of Inas and Ishwar, the mill flourished, generating substantial profits. The duo worked tirelessly, day and night, turning Rukkayya Shanubhog's dream into a thriving reality. Inas, through his hard work and dedication, earned a decent income and enjoyed a comfortable life. Antony and Narayan were filled with pride and joy as they watched their sons grow professionally and personally.

For eight successful years, the business thrived. However, greed crept into Ishwar's mind. Over time, he began pocketing a larger share of the profits without informing Rukkayya.

One day, Inas confronted him. "This isn't right, Ishwar," Inas said anxiously. "You shouldn't be taking money out like this. What will happen if the owner finds out?"

Ishwar brushed him off casually. "Relax, Inas. Nothing's going to happen. Besides, what they're doing with this business is no different from cheating. I'm just securing my share. If you want, I can arrange a little something for you too," Ishwar suggested, attempting to rope Inas into his scheme.

"No!" Inas exclaimed firmly. "I don't want anything. I can't participate in such dishonesty. Jesus won't forgive me if I do." Inas remained steadfast in his integrity, steering clear of any illegal activities. His unwavering loyalty and humility earned him immense respect in the village.

By now, Inas had entered his prime and was considered an eligible bachelor. Marriage proposals started pouring in from neighboring towns and villages. After careful consideration, Inas chose Abrooze, the daughter of Saver, a well-respected resident of Chandaavara. Saver, known for his skill with a double-barrel gun, was often sought after by villagers to hunt monkeys that damaged crops.

Inas and Abrooze got married, and their life together was nothing short of blissful. Abrooze quickly adapted to Antony's household, winning everyone's hearts with her humility and dedication. She respected her father-in-law deeply and supported Inas in every way. A simple woman with no demands, Abrooze complemented Inas perfectly. Inas, in turn, adored her and ensured she was happy, often taking her on trips across the state.

In time, the couple was blessed with two children: Mary and Victor. Their house was filled with laughter and joy. Inas insisted that Antony close his tailoring shop and spend his days enjoying the company of his grandchildren. Life seemed perfect.

But happiness is often fleeting. One fateful day, Antony decided to revisit his shop to stitch a special bag for Inas. He poured all his love and effort into making it perfect. As he prepared to leave the shop, Antony leaned on his old Singer sewing machine, tripped, and fell. Tragically, the fall proved fatal, and Antony passed away on the spot.

As if that heartbreak wasn't enough, the oil mill that had brought prosperity to the family began to falter. Over the next two years, it succumbed to mounting challenges and eventually shut down completely.

It felt like all doors had closed on Inas. He was at a crossroads, uncertain of what to do. During this difficult time, his old friend Ishwar approached him with a proposal.

"Inas, this is the right time to make a change," Ishwar said. "I have a friend in Dubai who runs a massive business. He's agreed to give me a job. If you want, I can talk to him about you as well. We can go together and start a new life there. What do you say?" Ishwar looked at Inas expectantly.

Inas shook his head and politely declined. "No, Ishwar. Thanks for the offer, but I can't leave my family behind. I have responsibilities here that I cannot abandon. You should go ahead, though. I wish you all the best!"

Left to fend for himself and his family, Inas decided to venture into the coir business. He started making ropes and other essentials for farmers, selling them to make ends meet. It was hard work, but he and Abrooze poured their energy into the venture. Slowly but surely, they managed to scrape together a living. Life wasn't easy, but at least they didn't have to worry about their next meal.

Just as things were beginning to stabilize, tragedy struck once more. Abrooze suddenly fell ill with a fever that wouldn't go away. Despite Inas's best efforts to get her treated, she eventually succumbed to her illness and passed away. Inas was left heartbroken.

With the loss of his beloved wife, coupled with his daughter's failed marriage and his unemployed son's aimless existence, the weight of life's misfortunes bore down heavily on Inas. Yet, these challenges forged him into a man of resilience and inner strength.

Years passed. Inas's life eventually found a semblance of normalcy. He lived quietly with his daughter and granddaughter, finding joy in their company and simple daily routines. One morning, after dropping his daughter and granddaughter off at the bus station, he noticed two men approaching his house.

The men introduced themselves as associates of Ishwar, who had returned from Dubai after several years and was now a wealthy man.

"Ishwar has invited you to his home," one of the men said. "He sent us to bring you."

They escorted Inas in a luxurious car to Ishwar's residence. The house, named "Narayan," was nothing short of majestic. Ishwar was waiting at the door, and the moment he saw Inas, he rushed to embrace him.

"Inas!" Ishwar exclaimed warmly, his face lighting up with joy. Inas couldn't believe his eyes. Ishwar had transformed into a man of affluence, adorned with a thick gold chain around his neck and diamond rings on every finger.

After exchanging pleasantries, Ishwar offered Inas some tea and began to speak. "Inas, I've heard about everything you've been through. It's truly heartbreaking," he said with genuine concern. Pausing for a moment, he looked directly at Inas and continued, "I want to help you."

Ishwar revealed that he now owned a thriving fish business with branches in Udupi, Kundapura, Bhatkal, and several other towns. "I have a job for you, Inas, if you're interested," he said. "It's simple work but pays well. You'd just need to deliver postal covers to some of my branches once a week. This job can ease your financial worries. Will you consider it?"

Inas couldn't comprehend why he was being asked to deliver postal covers. "Me? Why me? Don't you already have plenty of workers?" he questioned.

"I anticipated this response from you," Ishwar said, smiling. "Inas, I know you are a man of principles who never takes money for free. That's precisely why I want you to take up this job. Every week, my boys will come to your house with the letters. You'll take the Konkan rail in the morning, hand over the letters to the recipients at the station, and then catch the next train to return home," Ishwar explained. Without waiting for Inas's reply, he stuffed three 500-rupee notes into his pocket and sent him home, stating, "Your work begins next Saturday."

As expected, Ishwar's boys arrived at Inas's house early Saturday morning with the envelopes. Inas searched for a suitable bag to carry the covers securely. His eyes fell upon the bag his late father, Antony, had lovingly stitched for him. He picked it up, and tears welled up in his eyes as memories of his father flooded back. He felt immense pride for his father's craftsmanship and the bond they shared. This bag, stitched with care and love, became Inas's trusted postal bag. Every week, it carried the 'tapals'—the letters.

Inas followed the routine diligently. He would take the train, deliver the envelopes to someone waiting at the destination, and his task would be complete. Since he had a two-hour wait before boarding the return train, he decided to use this time to visit his son, Victor, whom he affectionately called Bala. Bala's room was nearby, and Inas planned to give him some money and, if time allowed, share a meal of fish curry with him.

When Inas reached Bala's room, he knocked on the door. However, there was no response. He knocked again, but still, there was no answer. Concerned, he assumed Bala might have been asleep. Peering through the half-open window, Inas was horrified by what he saw.

Bala and another boy lay on the ground, half-naked, cigarettes in their hands. The room was engulfed in smoke, and the stench was unbearable. Inas strained to hear their murmured conversation.

The boy with Bala said, "Take some more, Victor. We'll get more tapal tomorrow."

Initially, Inas was confused, but the mention of 'tapal' struck a nerve. Slowly, the horrifying truth dawned on him. His knees buckled, and he collapsed to the ground. He realized the letters he had been delivering were part of a drug-smuggling operation. Worse, his son was involved.

The weight of the realization crushed him, leaving him utterly shaken and distraught.

Inas regained his senses and decided to go to the cops. He noticed a vehicle with a red light on the top and followed it. He peeped into the vehicle and noticed a young police official. The police official sensed something was off the moment he saw this old man. He escorted Inas to the police station, gave him a glass of water, and asked him to tell him calmly what the matter was. Inas still had not come to his senses. He could not believe that his son was a drug addict and also the fact that Inas himself delivered those drugs. Inas suddenly felt the bag on his shoulder. He could not stand the fact that those drugs were inside the precious bag Antony had made for him. He immediately removed the bag from his shoulder and threw it away. The bag fell far away, on a thorny fence. Inas could hear voices in his head; he heard the voices of his wife, daughter, and granddaughter.

The young policeman was still waiting to listen to Inas. When the official prompted Inas again, Inas shouted "No" and ran towards the train station. He boarded the return train, and on reaching his village, he rushed towards the Church. He met Father Lobo and confessed everything. He fell at Father Lobo's feet and asked him, crying, "Father, was I wrong? Will God forgive me for this sin?" Father Lobo assured him that he had not sinned and that the Lord would definitely forgive him. He blessed Inas.

Do you think Inas heard his blessings? Inas fell over on the Father's feet and breathed his last. Father Lobo realized that he was no more and then requested the Lord to accept his soul saying, "May his soul rest in peace!"

5

THE JUDGEMENT

It was a Sunday morning. Sunlight streamed through the open window, brightening Arvind's face. The warmth of the sun disturbed his sleep and forced him awake. Struggling to open his eyes, he groggily muttered to himself, "Ah! I must have forgotten to pull the curtains last night."

Glancing at the clock, he noticed it was almost nine in the morning. Arvind rarely slept this late, even on Sundays, given his typically busy schedule. Occasionally, he worked on Sundays as well. Every two weeks, Arvind made it a point to visit his mother, who lived in Challakere. He would spend Sunday with her, stay the night, and leave for work directly from her home the next day.

The previous night, however, had been an exception. Arvind had stayed up late preparing for a special lecture titled "The Influence of English Literature on Kannada Neo Poets." Perhaps he would have slept longer had it not been for the persistent sunlight streaming through his window.

He was slated to deliver his lecture at an event where he was invited as a guest speaker. Arvind, an English lecturer at a reputed college, had earned his doctorate by the age of 36. He was fluent in both Kannada and English, making him an expert in both languages. Despite these extraordinary accomplishments, Arvind was known for his kindness, humility, and deep knowledge. His rich, harmonious voice and composed personality suited his profession, earning him immense respect among the intellectual elite.

As per his routine, Arvind had mentally rehearsed the key points of his speech before going to bed. His thoughts revolved around the structure of his lecture:

"There was a time when Kannada literature came to a grinding halt, teetering on the brink of losing its identity. At this crucial juncture, the poet B.M. Sri stepped forward, reconstructing Kannada language and literature while paving the way for neo-literature. His genius lay in rejuvenating Kannada poetry with a novel rhythm and a new dimension to its poetic form. Before B.M. Sri's era, poets like Narasimhacharya, Panje Mangesh Rao, and Hattiyangadi Narayan Rao had already laid the foundation for this transformation through their contributions to translation. These pioneers marked the birth of a new wave in Kannada poetry."

He continued, "Driven by their exposure to English literature, the Indian freedom struggle, and the rise of a new wave in journalism, these poets became aware of developments in Kannada literature. Later, Kannada poetry was further enriched by the disciples of B.M. Sri, such as Ku Vem Pu, Masthi Venkatesh Iyengar, and V. Seetaramaiah, whose works are treasures we still cherish today."

Recalling his speech brought a smile to Arvind's face. The lecture had been a resounding success, earning applause and accolades from the esteemed audience of scholars. His well-substantiated arguments had deeply moved the attendees, leaving many emotionally stirred as he concluded his talk.

When Arvind stepped off the stage, he was greeted warmly by many people who expressed their appreciation for his insightful speech. Among them was a young lady, likely around the same age as Arvind, who seemed particularly impressed by his lecture.

"Congratulations, Sir. You were fantastic today," she said. "I'm also a student of literature. My uncle, Prof. Hemanth Dharwadkar, has told me a lot about you."

Hearing her mention Prof. Hemanth Dharwadkar, Arvind's guide during his doctoral studies, brought a smile to his face. He held immense respect for his mentor and immediately inquired about his well-being.

"He's doing alright now, but he recently had a cardiac arrest. Thankfully, he's recovering well and is staying with his son in Miraj," the young lady informed him.

The news saddened Arvind, and he resolved to visit his professor at the earliest opportunity. Before he could dwell on the thought, the young woman interrupted, saying, "Would it be alright if I asked for your phone number? I'd love to seek your guidance on my thesis."

Arvind gladly shared his contact information, assuring her that he would be happy to assist her.

The next morning, as Arvind finished washing up, his maid, Shankaravva, had already prepared the milk and set breakfast on the table. Arvind had come to know Shankaravva through his landlord, Ekantappa, for whom she also worked. Recognizing her reliability, Arvind had arranged for her to cook his meals—breakfast, lunch, and dinner—and paid her promptly for her services.

On this particular morning, however, Arvind noticed that his landlord, Ekantappa, entered the house right behind Shankaravva. At that moment, Arvind remembered it was rent-payment day.

"I'm not here for the rent," Ekantappa said with a grin as he made himself comfortable in a chair. "I wanted to talk about my daughter, Lakshmi. She's grown very beautiful these days, don't you think?"

Caught off guard, Arvind hesitated before replying. "Umm, yes... she has. I've noticed," he said, unsure of where the conversation was headed.

When Arvind had first secured his job as a lecturer at Durga College, he needed a place to stay near the institution. After his father's passing, Arvind's mother, a retired schoolteacher, had decided to live with her own father in Challakere. Although Challakere was only 40 kilometers away, commuting daily was not feasible for Arvind due to his physical limitations. Having suffered from polio as a child, Arvind had lost strength in his left leg, making long journeys particularly taxing. Additionally, his mother had suffered a paralytic stroke, which required her to remain under the care of a caretaker at her father's house.

With no alternative, Arvind had to rent a house near the college. A colleague had mentioned an available room at the home of Ekantappa, who worked as an overseer in the Public Works Department. Upon learning that Arvind belonged to his community, Ekantappa readily offered him the room. He even went the extra mile, helping Arvind with food, laundry, and other necessities.

Over time, Arvind grew comfortable in his new accommodation and appreciated the landlord's willingness to assist him in settling down. However, this morning's conversation about Lakshmi left Arvind wondering what exactly his landlord had in mind.

Many times, Arvind had to visit his landlord's house to collect his room key, as the maid, Shankaravva, cleaned his room after he left for work. Otherwise, he rarely had any reason to interact with them.

One day, Arvind found himself in such a situation. He needed his room key and headed to the owner's house. He rang the doorbell several times, but no one answered. Curious and slightly impatient, he peered through the half-open window. Inside, he saw a girl sitting in an odd position. She looked lifeless, her gaze fixed on some distant point, completely unresponsive.

"Hello?" Arvind called out, hoping to get her attention. She didn't even flinch. The eerie stillness in her demeanor unnerved him.

Just as he tried to make sense of what he had seen, he heard Shankaravva's voice from behind. "Sir... Sir!" she shouted, hurrying toward him with the room key in hand.

"When did you come, Sir? I hope you didn't have to wait too long," Shankaravva said, handing him the key.

Noticing the puzzled expression on Arvind's face, she added, "Oh, you must have seen Lakshmi, Sir. That's Ekantappa's daughter. She's... not mentally sound. She always has that dull look on her face."

Arvind wasn't entirely convinced but chose to let it go. He nodded, thanked her, and returned to his room.

Later that night, Arvind was surprised when Ekantappa came to his room. The landlord appeared troubled, his face shadowed with hesitation, as though he was mustering the courage to speak.

"Do you have something to tell me, Uncle?" Arvind asked, breaking the silence.

"Yes. Shankaravva told me you were at our house earlier this evening," Ekantappa began.

"Oh, yes, I was there to collect my room key. I didn't know you weren't home," Arvind replied.

"Yes... You saw my daughter, Lakshmi, didn't you?" he said, his voice heavy. He paused, his gaze falling to the floor, before continuing, "I... I have to tell you something, Arvind."

Arvind remained silent, sensing the gravity of what was coming.

"I've committed a crime," Ekantappa confessed. His voice trembled as he spoke. "One day, my wife and I were having a heated argument. Lakshmi walked in. I didn't even notice her at first. You'll hear about this someday, so I might as well be honest with you now."

He paused, wiping the tears that had started rolling down his cheeks. "I had an affair. It was a mistake. My wife found out, and even after I ended things, she wouldn't let it go. Every conversation turned into a fight about it. One thing led to another, and... and I hit her. I didn't mean to, Arvind. I wasn't thinking straight. It was a heated moment, and I slapped her across the face. She fell... and never got back up."

Arvind was stunned into silence as Ekantappa's voice cracked with emotion.

"My wife died that day, and I've carried the guilt ever since," Ekantappa continued, his tears now flowing freely. "Lakshmi... my poor Lakshmi... she walked in right as it happened. She had come to tell us about her B.A. results. She saw it all—the moment her mother fell and never woke up. It broke her. She screamed and then collapsed. When she woke up, she had lost her voice... and her mind. She hasn't been the same since. She doesn't speak, doesn't respond, and doesn't seem to comprehend what's happening around her."

Ekantappa moved closer to Arvind, desperation etched into his face. "I've tried everything, Arvind. Nothing has worked. I can't bear to see my daughter like this anymore. I want her back—the way she used to be. Please, Arvind, help me. Help me fix my daughter."

Overcome with emotion, Ekantappa hugged Arvind tightly, sobbing uncontrollably as he pleaded for help. Arvind stood frozen, the weight of Ekantappa's confession pressing down on him, unsure of how he could possibly offer the solace and solution the man so desperately sought.

All of this was too much for Arvind to digest. He didn't know how to react, so he quickly freed himself from Ekantappa's arms and said, "Uncle, I really don't know what to say. What can I say? How can I help? I truly don't know!"

Ekantappa left the room and closed the door behind him. Arvind felt that Ekantappa deserved no sympathy for his actions. However, he also realized that the important issue now was Lakshmi's health, not her father's misdeeds. "Lakshmi's life is valuable. Her life can't be destroyed," Arvind told himself. He decided on a course of action and resolved to execute it the next time he saw Lakshmi.

Whenever Arvind happened to come across Lakshmi, he greeted her and tried to start a conversation. "Hi, Lakshmi! How are you doing?" he would ask. However, his questions were always met with silence.

The second time he encountered her, he thought to himself that Lakshmi looked like a speechless beauty, resembling the intricate sculptures of Belur. This time, Arvind approached Lakshmi, sat down beside her, and spoke gently.

"Lakshmi, don't be scared. I'm also a part of your family. You can talk to me about anything, whenever you feel like it," he said.

Suddenly, Arvind noticed Lakshmi shivering and heard her murmur something indistinct. Then, all of a sudden, she rose from her chair, ran toward Arvind, hugged him tightly, and began to weep uncontrollably. Although Arvind's words couldn't seem to reach her fully, Lakshmi had found a friend in him.

Arvind began bringing books from the library for Lakshmi to read, particularly books written by female authors. Lakshmi seemed genuinely excited to read them.

Whenever Arvind saw Lakshmi, he made it a point to greet her warmly and ask how she was doing. To his delight, Lakshmi began responding, saying, "I'm fine. How are you doing?"

Although Lakshmi now seemed better outwardly, she still harbored a deep hatred for her father. Her fiery eyes and cold stares toward him made this abundantly clear.

One morning, Ekantappa came to Arvind's house again. Repeating his earlier question, he asked, "My Lakshmi has improved a lot, hasn't she? What do you think of her?"

Arvind, caught off guard, responded hesitantly. "Um, yes, Uncle. She has, indeed. Please give these books to her," he said, handing over a collection of Neil Carnegie's works. He paid his monthly rent on his way out and walked away.

As he left the house and made his way to work, Arvind suddenly recalled his late father and found himself in tears. He realized that if his father were alive, he would be around the same age as Ekantappa.

Arvind's father had been a popular figure in Challakere, deeply respected by the entire village. He had led a simple, sincere, and compassionate life as a teacher. Always clad in a white dhoti, a long white shirt, a jacket, and a white cap, he embodied dignity and humility. Additionally, he had been well-versed in the Vedas and Upanishads, earning him further admiration.

'Everyone waited to listen to Arvind's father recite Gadha Yuddha, especially the episode where Bhima broke Duryodhana's thigh. He had lost three children, and even Arvind had lost a leg to polio. But Arvind's father was always optimistic. Not once did he cry over this fate. He would always console his wife, saying, "You see, God has at least given us one child. Let's take care of him now. We won't gain anything if we blame the Lord."

Arvind's father had enjoyed reading Rishi Aurobindo and Ramana Maharshi's books. He would also take Arvind to meet saints and writers to inculcate good culture in him. His father also took Arvind to meet Sirigere Swamiji and Sri Siddeshwar Swamiji and made Arvind touch their feet and receive their blessings.}

Arvind was in the final year of his postgraduate studies when his father passed away. Fortunately, Arvind had visited his hometown just a week prior to his father's passing. His father had walked him up to the bus stand and bid him farewell. That was the last memory he had of his father. Arvind always recalled his father's words, "Arvind, doctors and engineers are not the only ones who survive in this world. Teaching is a noble profession, my son. I want you to take up teaching and impart education and knowledge to youngsters. Also, when you are a teacher, you should never have 'money' on your mind..."

His father had been still in the middle of advising Arvind, but the arrival of the bus had cut him short.

Recalling those memories, Arvind thought to himself, "Father should have stayed around. He should not have died so early. I lost a rare opportunity of listening to the stories of Kumaravyasa, Mahabharata, and the fall of Duryodhana. If he were around, I also could have discussed Milton, Byron, Shakespeare, and so many other writers with him!" His eyes welled up, and the tears did not stop rolling down his cheeks.

* * *

In a span of a few days, Arvind received a call from Veena Dharwadkar. "I would like to meet you to get some suggestions on one of the subjects. Can I come to meet you tomorrow afternoon?"

"Oh yes, why not? My classes will be over by three o'clock. You can come over to the college, and we can discuss it. I'll share whatever little I know," Arvind replied.

The next day, Veena arrived at the college at 4:00 p.m. Arvind was surprised to see her in a completely different attire. When he had met her earlier, she had been dressed in western clothing. But that day, she wore a cream-colored saree with a saffron border, paired with matching jewelry. A bindi adorned her forehead, and to Arvind, she appeared as the epitome of beauty.

"Oh! You look like an angel…!" he exclaimed.

She gave a pleasant smile and responded, "Thanks."

"There are only two categories among women—one, a Goddess, and another, a doormat," Arvind thought to himself, recalling Pablo Picasso's famous remark. To him, Veena undoubtedly belonged to the first category.

"I wanted to get your suggestions on my study," Veena began, "I'm comparing the works of Dante and Akka Mahadevi. My focus is on their lives and their artistic contributions."

"Ah! You've chosen a fascinating topic," Arvind said. "Actually, anybody can be compared to anyone if you know your subject well," he paused. "I must admit, I haven't studied Akka Mahadevi in great depth. However, I do know that both she and Dante lived in the 12th century. I can certainly share some insights about Dante."

Arvind delved into Dante's Divine Comedy, explaining the epic's themes of heaven and hell, and its depiction of the journey towards the union of Atman and Param Atman. Veena listened attentively, noting down every detail in her diary, completely engrossed in the discussion.

After their prolonged academic exchange, Arvind arranged for some coffee and biscuits, and their conversation shifted to more personal topics. Veena hesitated for a moment before speaking. "I don't know whether you are aware, but I am married. I've been trapped in the cage of family life with a scientist husband for the past four years. He's a sadist, and I endure his torture every single day. I'm just waiting to be freed from his shackles. I'm not an angel, as you earlier said… I'm actually just a doormat…" Her voice cracked, and she stopped to wipe away her tears.

Feeling uncomfortable, Veena shook Arvind's hand, thanked him, and left abruptly. Arvind, too stunned to respond, simply stood there, watching her walk away. His mind was clouded with confusion and empathy.

Just then, he heard a voice behind him. "Who's that lady? She's the most beautiful woman I've ever seen. Someone like you could never land her," sneered one of his colleagues, mocking Arvind's physical disability.

Disgusted by the comment, Arvind shot him a cold glare and walked away without uttering a word.

Sometimes, Arvind could not help but dwell on such hurtful comments. He wished he could forget what he had heard, but the words lingered, gnawing at him. In an attempt to distract himself, he recalled a special Diwali advertisement he had seen recently. It was an announcement for a writing competition—an opportunity for writers to explore new forms of storytelling and experiment with their craft.

Arvind had always been deeply interested in newspapers, magazines, and literary articles. Becoming a reputed name in the field of literature had always been his dream. That evening, he decided to work on writing his "special story" for the competition. He wanted to steer clear of common topics like politics, social taboos, and societal atrocities. Instead, he yearned to explore a new writing style and a completely unique subject.

Suddenly, Veena came to his mind. Her story and the glimpse she had given him into her troubled married life had left a lasting impression. Arvind had often observed that a lack of trust and an inflated sense of personal prestige were major causes of discord in modern marriages. Drawing inspiration from Veena's story, Arvind decided to craft a narrative with her as the imaginative heroine.

He wove a unique story centered around a scientist, delving into the profound relationship between science and matter, the diligence and intellect involved in scientific pursuits, and the sensibilities required to navigate life's complexities. In the end, Arvind concluded the story with an insightful observation:

"Man is ruled by his emotions. When these emotions are deeply rooted in the heart, they provide a strong foundation for a fulfilled and meaningful life."

Pleased with his effort, he titled the story The Judgement. Satisfied with the outcome, Arvind felt a surge of happiness and retired to bed.

However, sleep evaded him that night. Veena's words kept echoing in his mind—the pain and vulnerability she had shared about her life weighed heavily on him. His thoughts soon wandered to the hurtful remark his colleague Mahendrappa had made earlier that evening. The sting of those words was fresh, and it cut deep.

Lying alone in his room, Arvind wept quietly. He longed for the comfort of his mother's lap, a place where he had always felt safe. Memories of his childhood crept in, and with them came the reminder of his crippled leg, the consequence of polio. He felt haunted by the thought of rejection—of women turning him away because of his disability. The weight of it all bore down on him, filling the night with a poignant loneliness.

* * *

Manoj took a walk around his residence that night, grappling with a whirlwind of mental disturbances and inner conflicts. These struggles had begun to seep into his professional life, affecting his performance at work. As a geologist, Manoj had a sharp eye for classifying samples collected from the mines, but lately, his focus had faltered. He found himself making mistakes in routine tasks, and his seniors had taken notice.

One day, an official memo arrived at his desk. A senior colleague, noticing the memo, remarked, "See, Manoj. You've been distracted lately. Your mind is elsewhere, caught up in writing stories, critiques, and participating in literary activities. Be careful."

Manoj felt a pang of frustration. He knew that his mistakes weren't because of his love for literature. "How can I make them understand my predicament?" he wondered. A science graduate by training, Manoj also had a natural talent for storytelling and poetry. His academic track record was impeccable, and many of his creative works had been published in prestigious magazines. Despite his full-time job as a geologist, Manoj had always found a way to balance his career with his passion for writing.

In fact, he was highly regarded in literary circles and was often invited to judge competitions. That very day, he had received a letter from a renowned newspaper, asking him to select the best stories from a list of ten finalists. Each story was unique, with its own charm, but Manoj successfully narrowed it down to the top three, evaluating them based on subject matter, depiction, and style.

One story, The Judgement, stood out. It captivated Manoj so much that he read it several times over three days. As he delved deeper into the narrative, he noticed something uncanny—it felt eerily similar to his own life. It was as though someone had been shadowing him, documenting his experiences in vivid detail. Certain passages mirrored specific incidents that had actually occurred in his life.

The story's depiction of a troubled marital relationship between a literature student and her scientist husband struck an especially personal chord. Manoj's own wife, Veena, was a literature student, and the dialogues in the story were almost identical to arguments they had had just days ago.

The unsettling similarities made Manoj suspicious. He began to wonder if Veena was having an affair with the story's author. Furious, he contemplated calling the writer to confront him, but he quickly realized his thoughts were clouded by anger. He took a deep breath, trying to calm himself, and reflected on the early days of his relationship with Veena.

They had first met in Dharwad during the All India Kannada Literary Meet. It was love at first sight. They courted for a while before eventually tying the knot. Their marriage, however, had been a mix of intense love and equally intense strife. Over time, their relationship had become strained, and they had drifted apart emotionally and physically.

Manoj picked up The Judgement and read it again. This time, he saw Veena as Amrutha, a character from S. L. Bhairappa's novel Anchu. Among the story's many thought-provoking observations, one line stood out to him:

"Science helps you identify a way of life and provides you with a vehicle to proceed. But it is left to you to find your own destination."

The words resonated deeply. Manoj realized that he had been so consumed by external expectations and internal conflicts that he had neglected his inner self. "Where did I falter?" he asked himself. He sat in deep introspection for hours before finally rising from his desk and walking out of the room. The story lay open on his desk, its narrative mirroring his own life, and a whole can of worms had been unleashed in Manoj's mind.

Epilogue:

Do you want to know what happened next?

1. Arvind got engaged to Lakshmi, and they set a date for their wedding.
2. Manoj called his wife, Veena, and invited her to return to their home in Bellary. He took the first steps toward mending their relationship.
3. Arvind's story The Judgement won first place in the writing contest.

6

THE BALLOON

Mumbai is a city that never sleeps. Mumbaikars start their days early and end them late into the night. With long distances to cover for personal and professional reasons, people often have to leave at least two hours early to ensure they reach their destination on time.

It's safe to say there's never a dull day in Mumbai. However, on this particular day, the city seemed unusually gloomy. Loud cries echoed through the air, and a sense of fear and unease clouded everyone's faces. At dawn, an unusual crowd had gathered in front of a small hut nestled amid a cluster of houses in Bhairampadi's Khadi area in East Bandra. Clearly, something unfortunate had happened.

This gathering was considered 'unusual' because Mumbaikars rarely stop to gather unless it's for something significant. Even the Mumbai police are known for their delayed response unless the matter is of great urgency. Therefore, it was evident that the situation was intense.

As it turned out, Gulabi and Santya's 19-year-old son, Raju, had been missing for the past three days. Gulabi, deeply attached to her son, was inconsolable. She cried uncontrollably while neighbors gathered around to offer their support. Her husband, Santya, though equally distressed, was too unwell to express himself.

Raju was a young boy who sold balloons to help his family with the little money he earned. He was well-liked in the community. However, as news of his disappearance spread, speculative and sometimes harsh comments began surfacing in the crowd.

"He must have gone off to watch Amir Khan's film shooting," one person said dismissively.

"No, I think he's just wandering around, chasing girls. Give it two days; he'll come back on his own," added another.

These insensitive remarks only added to Gulabi's grief. She felt helpless, her heart aching for her son's return.

Despite the negativity, women from neighboring huts tried to comfort her. "Don't worry, Bhabhi. He will definitely come back soon. Allah is listening to our prayers," they said, their voices filled with genuine empathy.

One positive aspect of this slum was its communal harmony. People from various religions lived together peacefully. The area, known as Zakaria Nagar, was predominantly home to Muslim families, but Hindu families were also an integral part of the community. During Muslim festivals, dishes like Surkumba and Mutton Sukka were shared with everyone, including Hindu neighbors. Similarly, during Hindu festivals, delicacies like Obbattu and Puliyogare were distributed among all.

Amidst this harmonious community, Gulabi and Santya decided to lodge a police complaint when no one could determine Raju's whereabouts. Since Santya was unwell, Gulabi had to take charge. Many men in the area whispered criticisms, labeling Gulabi as the dominating one in her household. However, Gulabi paid no heed to their remarks. Her sole focus was to find her son.

As they were preparing to visit the police station, a tall man with a stern expression entered the slum. He carried an air of authority that immediately commanded attention. This man was Dayal.

It wasn't the first time Dayal was visiting Gulabi's hut. He had made it a routine to visit them at least once a week. Raju worked at Dayal's balloon company, and Gulabi was employed as a maid at Dayal's house and three other apartments in his building.

Dayal hailed from Mughal Sarai in Uttar Pradesh. He had moved to Mumbai at a very young age and started as a laborer in a mill. Over time, he pursued some education and became an avid reader. His leadership qualities surfaced when he actively engaged in organizing a union for mill workers. During a major workers' strike, Dayal established himself as a prominent leader. However, after the closure of the Mumbai mills, he started a balloon factory and settled in Kalanagar. Despite being sixty, Dayal maintained a strong physique and lived a disciplined life. He cooked for himself, lived alone, and occasionally traveled, though he never stayed away for long.

Gulabi had been entrusted with a duplicate key to Dayal's house to carry out her daily chores. However, his personal room was always locked, and only Dayal kept the key to it.

Raju admired Dayal deeply, treating him as a godfather. He was well aware of how Dayal financially supported his family, and this made him respect Dayal even more. Despite Dayal's genuine kindness, there were those in the slum who spread malicious rumors. Some slandered Dayal's frequent visits to Gulabi's hut, insinuating that he was fulfilling her physical needs, given that her husband was unwell. However, Gulabi paid no heed to these baseless rumors, and neither did Raju.

When Dayal entered the crowded slum that morning, everyone was taken aback. His presence commanded attention. Without hesitation, he approached Gulabi and advised her against filing a police complaint.

"I've already sent my men to search for Raju, Gulabi. Don't make the mistake of involving the police—it will only complicate things. Trust me, I will do everything in my power to bring him back," Dayal assured her. As a gesture of support, he handed Gulabi two thousand rupees before leaving the scene.

Gulabi, who had immense faith in Dayal, accepted his words as orders. She decided not to go to the police, trusting him entirely. With her now calmer demeanor, the crowd began to disperse, returning to their daily routines, including Aslam Bhai.

Sadly, months passed with no sign of Raju. Dayal's efforts to locate him yielded no results. People in the slum began speculating that Raju might have been murdered. This suspicion stemmed from an incident that occurred just days before Raju's disappearance.

Two government officers had visited the slum, announcing that the area would soon be demolished to make way for government offices. A blueprint for the project had already been finalized, and the proposal included relocating all slum dwellers to a rehabilitation center in Navigaon near West Dahisar.

When the officials arrived, accompanied by contractors, Raju, brimming with youthful determination, confronted them. He argued vehemently, opposing the demolition plans. "We will never leave this place! The rehabilitation center is too far from our workplaces. Not even God can force us out of here!" Raju declared boldly, earning the displeasure of the officials.

He had declared, "We will not leave this place, even if I lose my life." His defiant words deeply upset the contractors. Just a few days later, Raju mysteriously disappeared. Despite this, Gulabi never lost hope. She strongly believed that one day, her son would return to her. Though Dayal provided her with financial help, she couldn't stop worrying about what her beloved son might be enduring.

Santya and Gulabi loved Raju dearly. They nurtured him with immense care and pride, despite the hardships they faced. Although Raju was not exceptional in his studies, he always made his parents proud. He had completed his tenth standard in a local municipal school. However, his pursuit of further education was cut short when he joined Dayal's balloon company.

Dayal's company produced a wide variety of balloons, including shiny latex, mylar, and metallic ones. Raju, ever diligent, woke up early every morning to collect his stock of balloons and prepared to sell them. He worked at Bandra's 1.25-kilometre-long Band Stand Promenade, where he loved visiting landmarks such as the M. P. Theatre, Lovers' Lane, and the Western Coast. Among his inventory, the heart-shaped balloons were the most popular, particularly with newlyweds, couples, and young romantics.

Raju had a knack for creative marketing. "Place this balloon between your lips before you kiss each other, and it will touch your heart," he would say, endearing himself to his customers.

Every Sunday, Raju never missed a visit to Mount Mary Church. Here, he sold balloons adorned with portraits of Jesus and St. Mary. He had learned the art of persuasive speaking from Dayal, which made him a charming and effective seller. Additionally, every Thursday, Raju delivered balloons featuring Sri Sai Baba's portrait to the receptionist at Leelavati Hospital, who distributed them to ten patients free of charge.

Sometimes, Raju had to travel long distances within Mumbai, from Sanpada to Borivali, to sell decorative items like streamers, banners, and string balloons. These were used to adorn function halls for birthdays, marriages, and thread ceremonies.

Every night, after a hard day's labor, Raju returned home with a thoughtful gesture for his parents. He would bring snacks like Kurkure or vada pav, which his father figure Santya particularly enjoyed. Once a week, he treated them to fried fish and kaju fenny from Goa. Gulabi was especially overjoyed on Fridays when Raju brought her jasmine flowers—her favorite.

However, Santya was neither Gulabi's husband nor Raju's biological father. Gulabi's story had its share of heartbreak. She had been married to a man named Madho, and together they had shared a beautiful, happy life. Both Gulabi and Madho worked at the Hiranandani project site in Powai.

Tragedy struck one fateful day when Madho, while engaged in bar-bending work at the site, was struck by a falling slab. He died on the spot, leaving Gulabi devastated. She had lost the love of her life, and all the company offered her in return was a small compensation.

Despite her immense grief, Gulabi had no choice but to return to work the very next day. Survival demanded it. Even with a broken heart, she pushed through her pain to provide for herself and her young son, Raju.

One day, as Gulabi was returning home from an exhausting day of work, she was ambushed by a group of goons and dragged to a dark corner of the road. Despite resisting with all her might, she was overpowered. The men subjected her to a horrific assault, forcing her to strip and raping her. After their monstrous act, they left her lying on the ground, broken and bleeding, for the entire night.

It was Santya who found her the next morning, lying in a pool of blood. Horrified, he immediately rushed her to a nearby hospital. Gulabi, thanks to Santya's relentless care, managed to recover physically in three days. However, the psychological scars ran deep. She could not recall much of the horrifying night—it was all a blur. But she knew something unimaginably terrible had happened to her.

After a thorough medical examination, the doctors revealed that Gulabi was pregnant. Santya, who had always been more like an elder brother to Gulabi, reassured her that he would stand by her no matter what decision she made. When Gulabi decided to keep the baby, Santya offered his unwavering support.

Although there were no romantic feelings between them, they decided to pose as husband and wife to avoid societal judgment and rented a small hut in Bhariampadi. Thus, they started living under the same roof.

Raju was born months later, and though he wasn't his biological son, Santya treated him with all the love and care of a devoted father. He did everything a father would do—providing for him, teaching him, and showering him with kindness. Despite living together, Gulabi and Santya respected each other's boundaries, sharing a bond built on trust and compassion. Santya's selflessness often moved Gulabi to tears.

When Santya fell ill, Gulabi took over his care without hesitation, tending to him with all the love and gratitude she felt for his years of kindness.

Days turned into weeks, and weeks into months, but still, there was no sign of Raju. While the rest of the slum slowly forgot and moved on, Gulabi couldn't. Every morning, she woke with the hope that her son would return. She prayed to gods from every religion, seeking divine intervention to bring him back.

One day, just before dawn, as East Bandra still lay in slumber, Gulabi heard a voice outside her door. The voice was faint yet familiar. Half-asleep, she struggled to recognize it. Then, as she listened carefully, realization struck—it was her son Raju!

"Aayi... Aayi..." Raju's cries filled the air.

Gulabi rushed outside and froze in shock at what she saw. Raju stood before her, a shadow of his former self. His face was clean-shaven, but he looked frail, with burns and bruises covering his body.

Overcome with emotion, Gulabi screamed in horror at the sight of her son's condition. Raju, barely able to stand, collapsed into his mother's arms. He gasped for air and, with great difficulty, began to recount his harrowing ordeal.

"Aayi," he whispered, **"I was kidnapped and taken to a dense forest. They forced me into training...I don't know what they were preparing me for, but I couldn't take it anymore. Somehow, I managed to escape. I reached the police station and told them everything I had witnessed."**

Exhausted and weak, Raju fainted in Gulabi's arms. Tears streaming down her face, Gulabi carried him inside and tended to him.

The next day, two major news flashes made headlines across the city:
1. The police had raided a terrorist camp deep within the forest, dismantling the operation.
2. Deen Dayal, a prominent figure in the slum, had surrendered himself to the authorities.

7

THE GENES

The sun had set hours ago, and the night had almost claimed the town when the KSRTC Airavatha bus arrived at Kumta Gibb's Circle from Mumbai. A man stepped down from the bus, his backpack slung over one shoulder, and glanced around, assessing his surroundings. His village was just one and a half kilometres away from the bus stop. He debated whether to walk or hire an auto. But first, he had a craving that needed satisfying—he wanted a steaming cup of chai.

Spotting a roadside stall named "Mahalasa," he felt a wave of relief wash over him. He approached the stall, ordered a tea, and sank into the moment as he savored every sip of the hot, refreshing beverage. The tiring journey had drained him, but the tea seemed to revive him. After paying the vendor, he stepped outside, feeling momentarily rejuvenated.

Suddenly, a loud voice pierced the calm evening.

"Arrey, Venkati! I've been waiting for you here by the road!"

Startled, he turned towards the source of the voice and immediately recognized it—it was Uncle Ganesh. The voice, filled with familiarity, carried a hint of urgency that made Venkati wonder why he had been summoned. Uncle Ganesh had telephoned him earlier, requesting him to visit the village for an important discussion.

As he approached Ganesh, Venkati scanned his face, hoping to discern whether everything was alright. To his relief, he didn't see any sign of grief or distress. It didn't seem like terrible news awaited him, but the lack of clarity gnawed at him nonetheless.

"Venkati, do you want a cup of tea?" Ganesh asked casually.

"No, Uncle, I just had one," he replied, trying to mask his impatience.

"Alright, let me get you a rickshaw."

Ganesh's relaxed demeanor only added to Venkati's confusion. 'If this was urgent, why isn't he telling me anything yet? What could it be?' he wondered, his thoughts swirling. Refusing the auto ride, he said, "No, Uncle. The village isn't too far. Let's walk."

Ganesh nodded and switched on his three-shell battery torch. The two began their walk towards Brahmur village, navigating the dusty, curvy road under the night sky. As they moved, the loose pebbles on the path clattered beneath their feet. While Ganesh led the way, occasionally reminding Venkati to watch his step, the younger man's mind raced with questions.

The silence between them stretched thin, filled only with the night's ambient sounds. Finally, Ganesh broke the quiet—not with the urgent topic that had brought Venkati here, but with unrelated chatter. He began discussing the gram panchayat's latest proposal to asphalt the road, the administration of Gokarna being handed over to Sri Mutt, and plans to build cattle sheds for the village's cows.

These were minor, almost irrelevant topics to Venkati, who was growing increasingly restless. 'What on earth is the urgency that brought me here?' he thought. He wanted to interrupt and demand answers, but he held back out of respect.

Ganesh wasn't a close relative. He had been their neighbor, a friend and confidant of Venkati's late father, Param Bhat. The two had once attended the same Sanskrit school to learn the Vedas, but their paths had diverged. While Param Bhat pursued the priesthood, Ganesh dropped out halfway and became an agriculturist. Local politics became his pastime, and he was known for his involvement in community affairs.

Despite their differing paths, Param Bhat and Ganesh had shared a deep bond. In the evenings, they could often be found sitting at the edge of the paddy fields, smoking beedis and exchanging news about their families. When Param Bhat had passed away unexpectedly, it was Ganesh who had taken charge of the final rites, ensuring they were performed at the Gokarna Pilgrimage.

But beyond these ties, Ganesh and Venkati had little interaction. This made Ganesh's sudden call all the more perplexing to Venkati.

As they walked on, Ganesh's seemingly casual demeanor did little to ease Venkati's mounting tension. 'Why isn't he getting to the point?' he thought, his patience wearing thin.

They continued down the winding road, the light from the torch illuminating their path. The clattering of pebbles beneath their feet echoed through the quiet night, as the mysterious purpose of Ganesh's call loomed larger in Venkati's mind.

Ganesh and Venkati finally reached the village. It was quite late by the time they arrived at Ganesh's house. As they approached, Venkati noticed Sharada atte sitting on the doorstep, her face lighting up with surprise when she saw him.

"Venkati! How nice of you to visit us. Is everything alright? What brings you here so suddenly?" she asked with genuine concern.

Venkati was taken aback. It was clear that Ganesh hadn't even informed his wife about summoning him with such urgency. This only deepened his confusion. Ganesh, sensing the awkwardness, quickly stepped in and answered on Venkati's behalf.

"Oh, he's here for some work," Ganesh said casually, avoiding further explanation.

After freshening up and changing into comfortable clothes, Venkati was offered some buttermilk and bananas by Sharada atte. The long, exhausting journey had left him craving rest more than food or conversation. He was just about to lie down when Ganesh appeared at the door of his room.

"Come on, Venkati. Let's take a stroll," Ganesh suggested, breaking the brief moment of peace.

"At this hour?" exclaimed Venkati, surprised and slightly annoyed.

"Yes," Ganesh replied, his tone insistent. "Come to the paddy field with me, please."

Venkati was speechless. He knew what Ganesh meant by the paddy field and couldn't help recalling his uncle's odd preference for relieving himself in the open rather than using a proper bathroom. Suppressing his irritation, he managed to mumble, "Can't it wait till morning?"

But Ganesh was adamant. "I know you wanted to rest, Venkati. Let's go; we'll be back soon. What I suggest is that you rest after dinner."

Resigned, Venkati reluctantly got up and followed Ganesh outside. As they passed through the garden, Sharada atte muttered under her breath, clearly unimpressed: "Why are they heading to the open field when we have two modern toilets in the house?"

The two men eventually reached the paddy field, the moonlight casting faint shadows on the path. Despite his annoyance, Venkati couldn't help but feel nostalgic about the days of his childhood when such trips were a common occurrence. Though the idea of squatting in the open disgusted him now, he begrudgingly joined Ganesh.

Ganesh, ever the chatterbox, began reminiscing. "Your father and I used to come to this very spot. It was our tradition to sit behind the bushes, share stories, and smoke beedis. Those were the days, my boy. After your father passed, I gave up smoking entirely. It just wasn't the same without him."

Venkati, by now, was at the end of his patience. His uncle's tangents about trivial matters, combined with the exhaustion from his journey, were wearing him thin. He could no longer hold back his irritation. Just as he opened his mouth to demand answers, Ganesh finally broke the suspense.

"Venkati, your father and I were very close," Ganesh began, his voice dropping to a more serious tone. "There's something I've kept hidden for years, something I promised to take to my grave. But now that your father is no longer with us, I feel it's time you know the truth. This secret has weighed on me for too long."

Ganesh's cryptic words only added to Venkati's frustration. "Uncle, will you please just get to the point? What are you trying to say?"

Ganesh took a deep breath, looked around as if to ensure no one else could hear, and continued.

"Your father..." he began, but his voice trailed off.

"What about my father?" Venkati demanded, his voice rising in impatience.

Ganesh glanced at him, hesitated, and then said, "It's about your lineage, your genes. There's something you need to know about where you come from."

Ganesh's words hung in the air like a heavy fog, suffocating and inescapable. Venkati felt as if the ground beneath him had crumbled. His mind raced with disbelief, anger, and a profound sense of betrayal. Yet, he remained silent, unable to process the whirlwind of revelations.

As Ganesh lit another beedi, the acrid smoke assaulted Venkati's senses, adding to the nauseating weight in his chest. He wanted to yell, to question, to demand answers. But he found himself mute, paralyzed by the enormity of what he had just learned.

"Your father isn't your biological father." The words echoed endlessly in his mind.

Ganesh continued speaking, his voice steady but laden with a mix of regret and justification.

"You must understand, Venkati. Your father, Param, was a good man, but after what he saw, something broke in him. He couldn't bear the betrayal, the humiliation. I tried to reason with him, but his anger turned inward. His health worsened, and he withdrew from everything. He hated the very sight of you, not because you had done anything wrong, but because you were a constant reminder of what had happened."

Ganesh paused, inhaling deeply from his beedi, the ember glowing in the darkness like a dying star.

"After your mother's death," he continued, "it was your grandmother who stepped in. She poured all her love into raising you, shielding you from the truth. She was a woman of great strength, and she never once let on about the storm that had engulfed this family."

Ganesh's voice softened, as though the weight of his confession was now bearing down on him. "I kept quiet all these years because I didn't want to burden you with this. But now… you're a grown man, living in the city, earning well. I felt it was time you knew the truth."

Venkati remained silent, his eyes fixed on the ground. His chest heaved with suppressed emotion, but he refused to let a single tear fall in front of Ganesh.

As they began walking back toward the house, Ganesh continued, perhaps mistaking Venkati's silence for acceptance.

"There's one more thing, Venkati. With your father gone and no other immediate family left, your aunt Nagaveni is all that remains of your connections here. She's been through a lot, losing her husband and living alone in hardship. She cared for your father in his final days, despite her own struggles. She could use some help."

Ganesh stopped walking and turned to face Venkati. "I know this is a lot to take in, but I believe we can do something good here. You don't have any legal claim to Parama's property since… well, you're not his biological heir. So I suggest this: let's go to Kumta tomorrow, sign some registration papers, and transfer the property to Nagaveni. She deserves it, and it will ease my conscience too."

Venkati's fists clenched at his sides, his jaw tightening. He couldn't believe the audacity of Ganesh to deliver such life-altering news and then immediately follow it up with a demand. The weight of the revelations and Ganesh's proposal churned in his mind like a storm.

He stopped in his tracks and finally spoke, his voice low and measured. "Uncle, I need time. This is too much for me to process right now. Let me think."

Ganesh nodded, seemingly satisfied that he had planted the seed. "Take your time, but don't take too long, Venkati. Decisions like this don't wait forever."

As they entered the house, Sharada atte was setting dinner on the table. The warm light from the kitchen felt strangely detached from the cold, heavy atmosphere enveloping Venkati's heart. He ate in silence, barely tasting the food, while Ganesh and Sharada chatted about trivial matters as though nothing had happened.

That night, as he lay on the hard cot in the guest room, Venkati stared at the ceiling, his thoughts a chaotic whirlpool. The truth about his lineage, the betrayal of his mother, the hatred of the man he had called "father," and now this sudden demand to give up everything—it was too much.

"Who am I?" he wondered. "What does any of this mean for my life now? And why should I have to pay for the sins of others?"

Sleep evaded him as he grappled with these questions, the weight of Ganesh's revelation pressing down on his chest like a boulder.

Venkati stood outside the house, staring blankly into the dark expanse of the night. The air was still, and the usual hum of the village felt eerily muted, as though even nature had paused to mourn with him. He gripped the cool bottle of water in his hand, hoping its chill could somehow soothe the firestorm raging in his heart and mind.

Each memory he had of Param now seemed tainted, fragile, and hollow. Was every affectionate moment with his father a lie? Had Param truly despised him all along? The very foundation of his identity had been ripped out from beneath him, leaving him flailing in a void of uncertainty. The realization that Ganesh knew the truth all along only added to the betrayal.

"Did Ganesh mock me in his heart every time I performed my father's rites with devotion?" he wondered bitterly.

The memories of people praising him as the epitome of a devoted son during Param's funeral now felt like cruel irony. He recalled how he had stood resolute, performing every ritual meticulously, his heart filled with genuine respect for a father he now realized had never truly embraced him.

As he walked further into the open field, his feet dragging along the dusty path, his thoughts shifted to the diary of the Malayalee pundit whose last rites he had performed a month ago. "Could that diary have held answers? Could he have been my real father?" The thought struck him like a lightning bolt, filling him with a fresh wave of regret.

"Why didn't I read it? Why didn't I look for answers then? Am I cursed to wander through life with questions that will never be answered?"

The pain in his chest tightened, making it hard to breathe. He sat down on a large rock near the edge of the field, gripping his head in his hands. The night's chill seeped through his shirt, but it barely registered. The weight of everything Ganesh had told him crushed him, and for a brief moment, he wished he could trade places with the silent stars above, devoid of thoughts, emotions, or pain.

As the hours crept by, the night deepened, and so did his despair. He replayed Ganesh's suggestion about transferring the property to Nagaveni. The material value of the property was insignificant to him, but the principle of the matter made his blood boil. How could Ganesh suggest he had no claim to the property, no place in this family, after everything he had endured?

And yet, amidst the chaos in his mind, a sliver of guilt pierced through. Nagaveni was indeed a widow, living alone in hardship. She had taken care of Param in his final days, showing him kindness and devotion. But why did this responsibility fall to him? He felt trapped, obligated to bear the burdens of a family that had rejected him from the very beginning.

Suddenly, a faint bark broke his thoughts. The two dogs that had barked earlier now approached him cautiously, their heads tilted in curiosity. One of them sat beside him, its warm fur brushing against his leg. For a brief moment, their silent presence was oddly comforting. It was as if they understood his pain in a way no human ever could. He reached out and patted the dog's head, finding a semblance of solace in its unwavering loyalty.

The first rays of dawn began to streak across the sky, signaling the start of another day. But for Venkati, it was hard to imagine life ever feeling normal again. He knew he couldn't avoid Ganesh's demands forever. The morning would bring yet another confrontation, another wave of questions, another reminder of his shattered identity.

As he stood up to return to the house, he whispered to the dogs, "At least you don't judge. At least you don't lie."

The walk back felt endless, his legs heavy with exhaustion. The quiet village, still asleep, seemed indifferent to the storm that raged within him. When he finally reached the house, he found himself pausing at the doorstep, reluctant to go back inside. It was no longer a place of refuge—it was now a symbol of all he had lost.

But life, he realized, wouldn't wait for him to process his pain. Tomorrow would come, with its questions and demands, whether he was ready for it or not. With a deep sigh, he pushed open the door and stepped inside, bracing himself for whatever lay ahead.

After the formalities were completed, Venkati felt a strange emptiness in his heart. The land that once symbolized his roots, his heritage, and the bond with his father—even if now revealed to be a lie—was no longer his. It was as though a part of his identity had been erased with every signature he had scrawled on the papers.

Nagaveni, still wiping her tears, looked at him and said, "You've done a great thing, Venkati. God will bless you for your sacrifice." Her words echoed hollowly in his ears. He nodded mechanically, avoiding her gaze, as he realized how little her blessing or gratitude meant to him at that moment.

Ganesh, on the other hand, seemed to have a sense of satisfaction. He spoke cheerfully to the sub-registrar and Nagaveni as though he had accomplished something significant. To him, this was just another task checked off his list.

The return journey to the village was quieter than the walk to Kumta. Ganesh tried to start a few conversations about local politics and other mundane matters, but seeing no response from Venkati, he gave up. The silence between them stretched unbearably, broken only by the sound of their footsteps.

When they reached the house, Sharada atte noticed the change in Venkati's demeanor. She served him lunch and tried to engage him in small talk, but he ate in silence. Even the simplest act of eating felt like an ordeal. The flavors of the food, which would once remind him of his childhood, now felt bland and lifeless.

After lunch, Ganesh asked, "So, what are your plans now, Venkati? Will you stay here for a while or head back to Mumbai?"

Without thinking much, he replied, "I'll leave tonight. I need to get back to work."

Ganesh nodded, though he appeared disappointed. Sharada atte looked concerned but said nothing. She packed some snacks for him to take on the journey and silently prayed for his peace.

That evening, as the bus rumbled along the winding roads back to Mumbai, Venkati stared out of the window, lost in thought. The countryside rolled past him, but he barely noticed. His mind was a whirlwind of emotions—anger, betrayal, sadness, and confusion.

"Who am I really?" he thought. The revelation about his birth, the loss of his land, and the sense of abandonment from both his parents and relatives weighed heavily on him.

For the first time, he began to question everything he had believed in. His identity, his purpose, and even the idea of family seemed blurred and uncertain. He had always been proud of being a Bhat, a lineage deeply rooted in tradition and respect. But now, that pride felt misplaced. "If I wasn't really a Bhat, then what am I?"

He thought about his mother—the woman he barely remembered. Her face, her voice, her warmth were all distant memories, clouded and unclear. He wished he had known her better, had asked questions, had understood her pain. But she was gone, leaving him with nothing but unanswered questions and a deep void.

As the bus neared Mumbai, the city lights came into view. For a moment, they seemed almost welcoming. Mumbai was chaotic, indifferent, and full of people who cared little about who you were or where you came from. Maybe, just maybe, he could start anew there—without the weight of his past, without the burdens of heritage, and without the chains of expectations.

That night, as he stepped off the bus and made his way to his small rented room, he resolved to focus on the present. The past, with all its bitterness, would remain in Brahmur, where it belonged. His life, his future, would be his to define.

For the first time in his life, Venkati allowed himself the freedom to dream—not as the son of Parameshwar Bhat, not as a Brahmin bound by tradition, but simply as himself.

Under the shade of the honne tree, Venkati reflected deeply on the twists and turns of his life. The searing heat of the Kumta seashore mirrored the turmoil within him. Though his immediate hunger was sated, his heart remained heavy with unanswered questions and unresolved emotions. Ganesh's sudden reveal and his insensitive behavior weighed heavily on him. The property was never his real concern; it was the betrayal, the timing, and the callousness that cut him deeply.

"Why now?" he wondered. "Did Ganesh think I would refuse to part with the property if I hadn't known the truth? Or was it just a convenient excuse for him to unload the burden of the secret he had carried for years?"

Memories of the past flooded back. Years ago, when he had left his maternal uncle Narayan after their heated argument, he had taken nothing with him—not even his matriculation certificate. The bitterness of their fight had been enough to sever all ties. With just a small amount of money he had earned from selling areca nuts in the local market, he had set out on an uncertain journey.

When he reached Chitrapur during the annual mela, he had no clear destination. The vastness of the fair only made his sense of directionless isolation more acute. He spent the night at a mutt, unsure of what the next day would bring. That was when he first encountered Vasanth Bhat, the priest who would become a pivotal figure in his life.

Vasanth Bhat's serene presence had been like a beacon of hope. The priest had noticed the distress in the young man's face and gently guided him to a guest room reserved for a special visitor. That visitor turned out to be Bijjur Saheb, a director of Corporation Bank, who had come to Chitrapur for the mela with his family.

Bijjur Saheb had been searching for a reliable attendant to help with the daily tasks at his residence in Mumbai. When Vasanth Bhat introduced him to the desperate yet earnest young man, Bijjur had taken an instant liking to him. The "interview" was more of a casual conversation, and to Venkati's immense relief and fortune, Bijjur offered him the job.

The years in Mumbai became transformative for Venkati. At Talamakki Wadi, he worked diligently and earned the trust of Bijjur Saheb and his family. They treated him not just as an employee but as a part of their household. He learned to manage responsibilities, adapted to the bustling life of the city, and even gained a sense of belonging he had never felt before.

Bijjur's daughter, in particular, had been kind to him. She shared her books with him, encouraged him to read, and inspired him to educate himself further. It was through her influence that he discovered his knack for organizing events, handling logistics, and even teaching younger children in the neighborhood.

As these memories surfaced, they brought both comfort and a sense of loss. The warmth and acceptance he had found with Bijjur's family were in stark contrast to the cold and calculated behavior he had experienced from Ganesh. He felt an even deeper sense of gratitude toward people like Vasanth Bhat and Bijjur Saheb, who had seen his potential when he was at his lowest.

Looking out at the sea, the waves crashing against the shore seemed to mirror the ups and downs of his life. "My roots may have been shaken, but I am still standing," he thought to himself. He realized that his identity was not confined to the secrets of his birth or the land he had signed away.

"I am who I choose to be," he whispered under his breath, feeling a renewed sense of purpose.

That evening, as he prepared to return to Mumbai, he resolved to focus on the future. The revelations of the day would take time to process, but they would not define him. He decided to pour his energy into his work and perhaps even pursue the education he had once abandoned.

Mumbai, with its endless possibilities and anonymity, felt like the right place to rebuild himself—not as the son of Parameshwar Bhat, but simply as Venkati, a man determined to create his own legacy.

As they say, God works in mysterious ways. Despite the upheavals in his life, Venkati had been fortunate to find mentors and guides who shaped his journey. Thanks to Bijjur's unwavering support and guidance, he eventually secured a position at Corporation Bank, achieving a sense of stability and self-reliance. However, life had more in store for him.

Through his work in Mumbai, he grew acquainted with Acchanna, a well-known caterer revered among Kannadigas for his excellent food quality. Acchanna's business was unmatched, whether it was weddings, thread ceremonies, birthdays, or engagement functions. His expansive house in Mulund, with a large adjacent shed capable of preparing food for up to 5,000 people, served as the hub of his catering empire.

Despite his professional success, Acchanna was known for his humility and work ethic. He had married a Marathi woman and had a daughter, Madhuri, who was of marriageable age. Whenever he had spare time, Venkati worked alongside Acchanna, learning the ins and outs of the catering business. Over time, his dedication and reliability earned him the position of Acchanna's right hand.

A turning point came when Acchanna suggested that Venkati leave his regular job at Corporation Bank and join the catering business as a partner. By then, the catering enterprise had expanded as far as Dahisar, becoming a significant player in Mumbai's competitive market.

Under Acchanna's mentorship, not only did the business flourish, but so did Venkati's financial situation. He had grown affluent enough to spend freely, but money alone didn't define his life. He valued the bond he shared with Acchanna, who was more than a mentor—a father figure.

Tragedy struck one fateful day. While preparing food for a 5,000-person event, Acchanna suffered a fatal cardiac arrest. Although Venkati rushed him to the hospital, it was too late. The loss left an indelible void in his life.

Inheriting the business after Acchanna's death, he became its sole proprietor. Yet, despite the financial security, he felt a deep sense of emptiness. Losing a mentor like Acchanna was akin to losing a part of himself. Recognizing the need to ensure continuity and to honor Acchanna's legacy, he decided to marry Madhuri, the late caterer's only daughter, and take responsibility for her family.

The marriage, however, did not bring the happiness he had hoped for. Though they were blessed with a beautiful daughter, Ambika, who quickly became the light of his life, his relationship with Madhuri was strained.

Ambika adored her father, and their bond was one of pure love and trust. She insisted on hearing her father's good-night wishes before she could sleep. The joy she brought to his life couldn't make up for the emotional distance he felt from his wife.

Madhuri, unfortunately, was not the supportive partner he had envisioned. Influenced by her mother's toxic remarks, she often treated Venkati with indifference or outright hostility. Instead of focusing on building a harmonious relationship, she allowed her insecurities and prejudices to poison their bond.

While reflecting on his life under the shade of the honne tree on Kumta's seashore, a phone call snapped him out of his reverie. It was Madhuri, her tone sharp and impatient.

"Where is the passbook? Where have you kept it? Tell me now!" she barked, not even bothering to greet him or inquire about his well-being.

The harshness of her voice brought him back to reality. Her lack of warmth stung deeply. She hadn't asked how he was doing, if he had reached the village safely, or even if he had eaten. Her words only deepened the resentment that had been simmering in his heart.

He sighed heavily, feeling like a beast of burden tied to an endless grindstone. He longed for love and understanding but received neither. As much as he wanted to bridge the gap in their relationship, he often felt as though his efforts were futile.

Still, despite the challenges, he resolved to keep trying—for Ambika's sake, if nothing else.

As soon as Venkati disconnected the call, his thoughts spiraled back to the day he had left for his hometown. That memory was vivid and unsettling.

He had returned home early that evening, only to find his wife, Madhuri, sitting unusually close to her music teacher, a Kashmiri Pandit. Though the sight felt inappropriate and gnawed at his heart, he chose not to react. Instead of confronting her or allowing his mind to speculate further, he quietly entered his room, packed his bags, kissed his daughter goodbye, and left. Madhuri's reaction—or lack thereof—didn't matter. Life had become too suffocating, and he desperately needed space to breathe.

As he reflected on his life now, sitting under the honne tree on Kumta's seashore, he longed for clarity, peace, and freedom from the emotional turmoil. He wondered: Was anyone in this vast world truly content? Could the losses of life ever equate to its gains?

By the time he reached Brahmur that evening, it was late. He avoided any unnecessary interactions, eating only a banana and drinking a cup of milk before heading to bed. Ganesh, sensing his mood, didn't insist on anything further.

For the first time in what felt like ages, Venkati had a good night's sleep. He forced his mind into a state of numbness, temporarily free from the overwhelming thoughts that had plagued him.

The next morning, as he performed his daily rituals, he overheard Ganesh and Nagaveni in a spirited conversation. Their demeanor, particularly Nagaveni's newfound strength and cheerfulness, caught his attention.

From a distance, he could hear Ganesh saying:

"See, I've kept my promise and handed over the property to you. Now, it's your turn. Don't forget to transfer the adjacent areca garden to me."

Those words hit like a thunderbolt. They unraveled the tangled web of manipulation and deceit that had been meticulously staged. Ganesh's cunning plot had been laid bare.

Venkati smirked in disgust. He had no words for his uncle's betrayal and greed. Deep inside, he prayed that he would never have to see Ganesh's face again. Without revealing his emotions, he packed his belongings and prepared to leave.

A few hours later, as he was about to depart, he bid Ganesh a casual farewell in Kannada: "Hogi bartini," meaning, "I'll be back."

But his words carried a weight that Ganesh couldn't decipher.

That night, Venkati did not return. Days passed, and there was still no sign of him. Ganesh grew restless. Fearing the worst, he set out to search for his nephew in nearby wells, ponds, and surrounding areas. But his efforts bore no fruit.

Ganesh couldn't stop replaying Venkati's parting words:

"Hogi bartini…"

They echoed in his mind, each repetition accompanied by an unease he couldn't shake.

Was it a simple goodbye? Or something more profound, more permanent? Ganesh would never know.

8

KUMPA SHETTY'S GANESH POOJA

It was the auspicious day of Ganesh Chaturthi in Kirki village's Naduchitte. Almost every household had already brought home their Ganesha idols, adorned and worshipped them, and even finished the festive meal. However, at Kumpa Shetty's house, things were different this year.

Kumpa Shetty, a renowned idol maker, was famous for crafting exquisite Ganesha idols every year. People eagerly awaited his creations, but this year was different. His health had deteriorated, and he could barely manage to complete the few orders he had received. Even the idol for his own house was still unfinished on the festival day.

Rukku, Shetty's bright and lively granddaughter, was growing restless. She had been eagerly waiting to see the finished idol and celebrate the festival. Running back and forth between the kitchen and the veranda, where her grandfather was laboriously painting the idol, Rukku finally let her frustration spill out.

"Grandpa! Everyone else has already offered their prayers and probably finished their lunch! The sweets are cold, and the fruits in the mantap are wilting, all waiting for your idol. Hurry up, please!" Rukku exclaimed, her tone both anxious and teasing.

Shetty, understanding her impatience, smiled apologetically. "I'm almost done, Rukku. Just a little more. I'll take a quick bath, and then we can do the pooja together. In the meantime, why don't you finish the eyes and add the final touches? You're better at that than I am."

Rukku's face lit up. Shetty always let her complete the eyes—a task that required precision and artistry. Painting the eyes of the deity was a sacred moment, believed to breathe life into the idol. It was a role Rukku cherished deeply.

Rukku loved painting, a talent she had inherited from her grandfather. She had learned advanced techniques from her art teacher, Nayak, who remained her mentor and biggest supporter. Just the previous evening, her rangoli of "Narendra Modi and Kashmir" in the local Gram Panchayat courtyard had won widespread praise. An entrepreneur from Mumbai had even rewarded her with ₹500 for her creativity.

As Rukku sat down on the veranda to paint the eyes, her hands moved skillfully, but her mind wandered. She couldn't help but feel concerned for her grandfather. His health had been failing, and this year, he had only managed to create two idols instead of the usual twelve.

Two major tragedies had taken a toll on Kumpa Shetty's health: his age and the loss of his daughter and son-in-law. Rukku's parents, Sunanda and Ratnakar, had died in a road accident while returning from a wedding. The memory of that day was still vivid in Rukku's mind—her grandfather's uncontrollable grief, the overwhelming sorrow that engulfed their lives.

Since then, Rukku had become Shetty's whole world. She had completed her Arts degree from Honnavar College and now stayed at home to help her ajja. She filled the silence in their home with her laughter and kept him motivated, even as his body grew frailer with each passing day.

As Rukku finished painting the eyes, Shetty returned, freshly bathed. His face lit up as he saw the completed idol. "You've done it again, Rukku! Our Ganesha looks alive and ready for blessings," he said, his voice filled with pride and love.

Together, they carried the idol to the mantap, adorned it with flowers, and offered their prayers. Though their family was small, their devotion was immense, and in that moment, Rukku felt a deep connection with her ajja and the traditions they upheld.

But in her heart, Rukku couldn't shake a question: Would this be the last Ganesha idol her ajja would ever make? She prayed silently, asking Lord Ganesha to bless her ajja with health and strength, so they could celebrate many more festivals together. After all, Shetty's art was more than just tradition—it was their bond, their legacy, and the heart of their home.

Rukku stared at the Ganesha idol after painting its eyes with delicate care and precision. A sense of satisfaction and pride lit up her face as she admired the finished work. Every idol created by her grandfather, Kumpa Shetty, shared a unique charm—each bore a serene, smiling face, was draped in red cloth, and featured a symmetrical trunk gently curved to the left. The crown shimmered under the soft light, and the bright, expressive eyes seemed to bring the deity to life.

Over the years, however, Shetty had to adapt his craftsmanship to meet changing preferences and modern techniques. This was one reason for the decline in demand for his idols. This year, he had only created two: one for his own home and the other for his neighbor, Nanappa of the Devendra Hegde family.

Nanappa, a solitary and God-fearing man, lived alone in his ancestral house. Although he hailed from a large joint family, tragedy had left him as the sole surviving member. Nanappa was deeply devoted to his faith, starting each morning by plucking bilva leaves from Shetty's compound and offering them at the nearby Ishwar temple. On every new moon day, he would pray at the Nagban and offer coconuts to Chowdi Devi, the Goddess Durga.

Nanappa was more than just a neighbor—he was a pillar of support for the Shetty household. It was through his influence that Rukku had secured a job at the local honey-produce cooperative society, earning a modest monthly salary of five thousand rupees. He often visited their house under various pretexts, bringing them fruits, sweets, or small financial help. Nanappa's presence reminded Kumpa Shetty of his estranged son, Manjunath, whose memory cast a long shadow over Shetty's life.

Manjunath was born after years of prayers and rituals, making him a cherished son. Shetty had hoped Manjunath would inherit the family business of crafting idols and managing their jewelry shop. To prepare him, he had sent Manjunath to Udupi to learn the trade, but the plan backfired disastrously. Manjunath began stealing jewelry from the shop, a betrayal that devastated Shetty. When the jewelry shop owner in Udupi discovered the theft, he sent Manjunath home with the stolen pieces and an escort as evidence. Enraged, Shetty lost his temper and beat his son black and blue.

Shetty had thought his anger was justified, but he failed to foresee its consequences. By the time he realized his mistake, Manjunath had run away, leaving a deep void in Shetty's heart.

Rukku gave the Ganesha idol a final, approving look and waited for her grandfather to join her. Shetty, however, was still in the bathroom. As it was already noon, there was no hot water left for his bath, and he had to make do with lukewarm water. Emerging from the shower, his frail body shivered slightly, and his face seemed more melancholic than usual.

"Ajja, what's wrong? You look so sad," Rukku asked, her voice tinged with concern.

Shetty sighed deeply. "I was thinking about Sunanda… your mother. I miss her so much today. And your father, Ratnakar, too. He was like a son to me, always looking after me and the family business."

Sunanda and Ratnakar's absence was a wound that never healed for Shetty. Sunanda had been a devoted daughter, and Ratnakar was a sincere man who had loved her deeply. He had been a dutiful son-in-law who helped Shetty run the jewelry shop with honesty and dedication. Their untimely death in the road accident had left Shetty emotionally broken and physically weakened, a shadow of the once vibrant man he used to be.

As Shetty's voice trembled with emotion, Rukku placed a comforting hand on his shoulder. "Ajja, they are always with us in spirit. And today, we'll offer our prayers to Ganesha, as they would have wanted."

Shetty nodded and gave her a faint smile. Together, they prepared to install the beautifully crafted idol in the mantap. For Shetty, the act of prayer became a way to channel his grief, finding solace in the rituals that connected him to his lost loved ones.

Shetty noticed the two men too, and though surprised, he didn't let it disrupt the pooja. He gestured for them to sit and join the ritual. After completing the arati, Shetty placed the bell down with trembling hands and turned toward the visitors. His silk attire, adorned with flowers and the holy marks of the pooja, made him look regal despite his frail health.

"Ajja, why is Nagesh here? And who is this with him?" Rukku asked softly, her tone filled with curiosity and concern.

Shetty gave a weak smile and said, "Rukku, let's hear from them directly." Turning to Nagesh, he added, "Welcome, Nagesh. It's been a while since I've seen you. What brings you here today, especially on this auspicious day?"

Nagesh, a robust man in his early fifties, stepped forward with a subdued expression. "Anna, I've come with a request, and I hope you'll hear me out without getting upset." He glanced at Rukku nervously and then continued, "This is Shivappa. He's my distant relative and a well-wisher. He has been visiting various families in search of a suitable match for his son, who's working in Bangalore. The boy is well-settled, has a good job, and comes from a respectable family. When I spoke about Rukku and her talent, Shivappa expressed an interest in meeting you."

Rukku froze in her place, her heart sinking at the sudden turn of events. She glanced at her grandfather, whose expression immediately darkened. "Marriage? For Rukku?" Shetty's voice was soft but laced with unease. He clenched his trembling hands into fists and looked away, struggling to contain his emotions.

Nagesh quickly stepped in to calm the situation. "Anna, please don't misunderstand. I only suggested this because Rukku is young, talented, and deserves a good match. This boy, from all accounts, is a gentleman who would treat her with respect and care. I thought it might bring some stability and happiness to her future."

Shivappa, standing awkwardly in the background, chimed in, "I understand this is a sensitive matter. I'm here with good intentions, and there's no pressure. If you wish, I can leave now and let you discuss this within the family."

Shetty shook his head, his voice cracking as he said, "Nagesh, I know you mean well, but Rukku is all I have left. She's not just my granddaughter; she's my only reason to live. How can I think of parting with her? Who will take care of me when she's gone? How will I manage?"

The weight of Shetty's words hung heavily in the room. Rukku stepped forward and placed a comforting hand on her grandfather's shoulder. "Ajja, please don't worry. I'm not going anywhere right now. Let's focus on the festival today. We can discuss this later."

Nagesh and Shivappa exchanged glances, realizing the depth of Shetty's attachment to Rukku. Nagesh rose to leave, saying, "Anna, I didn't mean to upset you. Take your time to think about it. Rukku's happiness is what matters most to us all."

As the two visitors left, the room fell silent except for the faint crackling of the oil lamp in the mantap. Shetty turned to Rukku, his eyes filled with tears. "You are my everything, Rukku. I don't know what I'll do without you."

Rukku knelt beside him, wiping his tears gently. "Ajja, I'm here now, and that's what matters. Let's focus on celebrating Ganesha's blessings today. We'll deal with everything else later."

They both returned to the pooja, the weight of unspoken fears and love thick in the air.

The return of Manjunath brought an unexpected wave of joy and closure to the family. Kumpa Shetty, who had spent years longing for his son, found himself overwhelmed with emotions. His frail heart, which had carried the weight of grief and regret for so long, now beat with a newfound vigor. As Manjunath bowed before him, seeking forgiveness, Shetty's eyes filled with tears of both relief and pride.

"Manjunath, my boy," Kumpa said, placing a trembling hand on his son's shoulder. "You've come back at the perfect time. Lord Ganesha himself must have blessed this reunion. I have no complaints anymore. The past is behind us. You've proved your worth, and that's all a father could ask for."

Rukku observed the scene with mixed emotions. Her once lonely grandfather now seemed vibrant, his spirit rejuvenated. For Rukku, the day brought a whirlwind of change—she not only met an uncle she never knew existed but also sensed a familial bond growing stronger with every passing moment.

As they sat for lunch, the warmth of family filled the house. The aroma of freshly heated dishes mingled with the scent of incense from the Ganesh pooja. Everyone seemed to be at ease for the first time in a long while.

Manjunath, visibly moved by Rukku's hospitality, couldn't help but compliment her cooking. "Rukku," he said warmly, "these dishes remind me of my mother's cooking. You've truly inherited her skills. You've made this day even more special for me."

Rukku smiled shyly, her cheeks turning a soft shade of pink. Manjunath's words were kind and sincere, but there was something deeper in the way he looked at her. Shetty noticed the exchange and chuckled softly, his wise eyes recognizing what was unfolding.

"Manjunath, you've missed a lot of years with the family," Shetty said, breaking the silence. "But perhaps, this Ganesh Chaturthi marks a new beginning for all of us. If the gods wish it, maybe our family will expand soon, and this home will be filled with even more joy."

Everyone laughed, but the underlying message wasn't lost on anyone. The festive spirit seemed to sparkle brighter, weaving its magic over the family.

After the meal, as the evening grew quieter, Rukku and Manjunath worked together to clean up. It was the first time they were alone since his arrival. "Rukku," Manjunath began hesitantly, "I hope you're okay with all of this. I know it's sudden, but I truly want to be here for you and Ajja. I've missed out on so much, and I'd like to make up for it."

Rukku, still processing the day's events, nodded. "Uncle, or should I say… Manjunath Anna, you've brought happiness back to Ajja's life. That's more than enough for me. I just hope you'll stay true to your word."

Manjunath smiled warmly. "I will, Rukku. I promise."

The night concluded with the family gathered in the living room, recounting old stories and making plans for the days ahead. Shetty, now visibly more energetic, looked around at the people he loved. "This is the Ganesh Chaturthi I've prayed for all my life," he said softly, his voice filled with gratitude.

The festival, once overshadowed by loss and longing, turned into a day of reunion, forgiveness, and newfound hope. For the Shetty family, this Ganesh Chaturthi marked not just the celebration of the Lord's blessings but also the beginning of a new chapter filled with love and togetherness.

9

POLARS MEET

The news of Parvatakka's upcoming visit to the United States to stay with her daughter for two months spread rapidly through the entire village of Neelkod, sparking diverse reactions among its residents. Some marveled at the idea of her traveling so far at her age, while others speculated on how the village would function in her absence. As a retired hospital matron who had dedicated her life to public service, Parvatakka was a beloved figure in the village and its neighboring areas. Affectionately called **"Nurse Parvatakka,"** she had turned her home into a makeshift clinic after retiring from her position at a hospital in Honnavar, refusing lucrative offers from private institutions in favor of serving her community.

Parvatakka's days were marked by discipline and devotion. She began her mornings promptly at six, completing her household chores before heading to her newly renovated meditation room. Situated on the right side of her home, this serene space was free from traditional idols and instead adorned with portraits of figures she revered: Mother Theresa, Ramana Maharshi, Samarth Ramdas, and Sri Shridhar Swamiji. At the center of the room hung an image of Brahma, symbolizing creation, gifted to her by the Brahma Kumari association. This room was her sanctuary, where she immersed herself in long hours of meditation, emerging with a calm and saintly aura that reflected her lifelong commitment to selfless service.

Clad in a pristine white saree, her Rudrakshi necklace complementing her tranquil demeanor, Parvatakka's presence radiated serenity. Many villagers likened her to a saint, a living embodiment of compassion and dedication. Her noble work and dignified appearance often made people wonder how stunning she must have been in her youth.

A Well-Managed Home

Parvatakka's household was modest yet inviting, known for its simplicity and charm. Her niece, Triveni, had moved in with her after completing her education. Triveni, who was the same age as Parvatakka's daughter Saraswathi, worked as a teacher in Saalakod village and took on the responsibility of preparing meals and managing the house. Their bond was one of mutual respect and support, with Triveni seeing her aunt as a source of inspiration.

The house overlooked a lush garden, accessible via ten stone steps, where areca, coconut, banana, and other fruit-bearing trees flourished under Parvatakka's meticulous care. Following the death of her husband, Subbaraya, she had taken over the garden's management, employing gardeners to assist her. The profits from the sale of fruits were never used for personal gain but were instead donated to local schools and charities, further cementing her reputation as a benefactor of the community.

Each morning, Parvatakka strolled through the garden, breathing in the fresh air and inspecting the trees. This daily ritual brought her immense peace and reinforced her connection to the land and its bounty.

Departure for the U.S.

The announcement of her journey abroad was met with curiosity and excitement. Villagers were keen to know how a woman so rooted in tradition would adapt to life in America. Would she embrace the modern conveniences of her daughter's household, or would she maintain her austere routines even there?

For Parvatakka, the trip was not just about visiting her daughter but also about experiencing a different culture. She saw it as an opportunity to reflect on her life's work and perhaps draw inspiration from her travels to enhance her service upon returning home.

As the date of her departure approached, the villagers, while eager for her to experience the world, couldn't help but feel a sense of loss at the temporary absence of their beloved "Nurse Parvatakka."

Every morning by 8:00 a.m., one could spot Parvatakka's reliable 'Hero Puch' scooty parked outside someone's house. Whether it was tending to wounds, removing sutures, or addressing any medical need, she was always just a call away, ready to serve. Her commitment to public service extended well into the afternoon. After her rounds, she would return home for lunch prepared by her niece, Triveni, and then take a brief but vital nap. The afternoon rest rejuvenated her for the second half of her day, which she spent conducting awareness camps. These camps emphasized blood donation and maintaining a healthy lifestyle.

Parvatakka was a household name in her village, beloved by locals and highly regarded by every doctor who knew her. Her selfless service, spanning thirty-two years, earned her genuine affection and respect. Even after retiring from her official duties, she continued to dedicate herself to the well-being of her community. The doctors admired her tireless efforts and often referred to her as an unsung hero.

A Legacy of Dedication

Parvatakka retired without a blemish on her impeccable career record. Though she was transferred twice during her tenure, the people of Honnavar, recognizing the value of her work, used their influence to ensure she remained in the village. Such was their attachment to her. Her dedication, compassion, and professionalism made her an irreplaceable figure in the community.

Unfortunately, life was not always kind to Parvatakka. She lost her husband at a young age but faced her challenges with unwavering strength and grace. Her dignified conduct and steadfast principles left no room for anyone to question her integrity. However, there was an incident during a medical camp that revealed the fiery spirit within her.

A surgeon attending the camp had crossed boundaries, attempting to harass her. But Parvatakka was not one to cower in the face of injustice. Grabbing her sandals, she delivered a resounding lesson, ensuring he regretted his actions. The incident spread like wildfire, reinforcing her image as a fearless protector of dignity and decency.

A Promising Journey to the U.S.

When her daughter invited her to visit the United States, Parvatakka's reputation for determination and straightforwardness came into play once again—this time during her visa interview. Her daughter had meticulously prepared all the documents and coached her on potential questions and answers.

Standing confidently at the yellow marker, Parvatakka faced Nancy, the Visa Officer, who began with a probing question:

"What guarantee do we have that you will return to India? You have a daughter in America, and she is your only child. What makes us believe you'll come back?"

Without hesitation, Parvatakka replied firmly, "I am a nurse from PM Modi's country. I have no need to render my services in your country. I have many patients waiting for me in India."

Nancy, taken aback by her conviction, responded with admiration. "Oh! That's amazing. You truly are the Florence Nightingale of the modern age."

Her visa was granted on the spot, no further questions asked.

An Unforgettable Hero

Parvatakka's life story resonated with those around her. From her relentless dedication to her profession to her boldness in standing up for herself and others, she was a beacon of hope and strength. Her trip to the U.S. was not just an opportunity to spend time with her daughter but also a well-deserved acknowledgment of her tireless service. For the villagers of Neelkod, she remained an icon of selfless devotion and indomitable courage.

* * *

Sam was restless and anxious as he waited in the lounge of the Mayo Clinic in Minnesota, USA. His face reflected a storm of unanswered questions, and his eyes were glued to the Neurology Department's operation theatre. He kept burying his head in his hands, sighing deeply, his body language betraying his unease. Unable to sit still, he got up frequently, his nerves on edge.

Finally, he noticed a doctor walking toward him.

"Sam, your son suffers from an aneurysm, a rare brain condition that requires immediate surgery," Dr. Bentley explained. "The surgery itself is not overly complicated, but managing the potential after-effects, like epilepsy, migraines, or memory loss, can be challenging. Dr. Deep, an experienced surgeon from India, is here. If you'd like, I can request him to perform the surgery."

Sam nodded, trying to process the news. His son, Robert, had recently been in a severe motorcycle accident, recovering after initial treatment. However, the intense headaches he experienced afterward had led them to seek medical help again.

After a moment's hesitation, Sam agreed to the surgery and gave Dr. Bentley his consent to contact Dr. Deep.

Soon after, Dr. Dipankar, known as Dr. Deep, arrived. A tall, fair-complexioned man in his early thirties, he exuded confidence and calm.

"I'm grateful for your trust, and I will do my utmost to ensure the success of this surgery," Dr. Deep said warmly. Looking at Sam, he added, "I understand your concern, Mr. Sam. I can only ask you to pray and remain calm. Everything will be fine."

Sam clasped the doctor's hands, his voice trembling. "Please save my son, Doctor. I have full faith in you."

To Sam, Dr. Deep seemed like a divine messenger sent to save his son. Quietly, he prayed, "Oh Lord, please save my Robert."

As Robert was wheeled into the operation theatre, Sam sat down, his thoughts drifting to happier times with his son. He replayed memories of Robert's smiling face, their father-son adventures, and the bond they shared. Then, a sharp flash of the accident scene jolted him from his reverie. Time crawled as he kept checking his watch. Four hours passed.

Finally, the doors of the operation theatre opened, and he heard the word "Successful." Dr. Deep, alongside his team, emerged, giving Sam a reassuring thumbs-up. The procedure had gone well.

Dr. Deep addressed the team, and his gratitude was evident. "This surgery was a success thanks to all of you. Thank you, Doctors. Great job!" He shared a warm smile with Dr. Saraswathi, the anaesthesiologist, who had worked tirelessly throughout the operation.

Inside the theatre, Dr. Saraswathi had been an indispensable part of the team. She meticulously monitored Robert's heart rate, breathing, hydration levels, and overall stability under anesthesia. Her sharp attention ensured that the patient remained stable during the critical phases of the surgery. After the operation, she performed a final check before Robert was moved to the recovery room.

As Robert was transferred, Sam's heart swelled with relief. His faith had been rewarded. He silently thanked Dr. Deep and his team, whispering a prayer of gratitude. The ordeal had brought him closer to understanding life's fragility—and its resilience.

After the exhausting surgery, Dr. Saraswathi heaved a sigh of relief and decided to take a break. She joined Dr. Deep outside the hospital, and together they walked to the nearby Starbucks. As they settled down with their orders—Dr. Deep with his hot cappuccino and a slice of pumpkin cake, and Saraswathi with her chai latte—they began discussing the events of the day.

Dr. Deep, who had recently transitioned from AIIMS in India to Mayo Clinic, shared his insights about the surgery. Saraswathi, who had completed her medical degree and postgraduation in anesthesia at Chandigarh Medical College, had been in the U.S. for only five months. Despite the short time, she had become an integral part of Dr. Deep's surgical team and admired his exceptional skill in the operating room.

"How does he handle the instruments so effortlessly?" Saraswathi often wondered. "It's as if he was born to be a surgeon."

As they talked, Dr. Deep's tone grew somber. "Subarachnoid hemorrhage," he began, "is when a burst artery in the brain causes blood to clot and exert pressure, often leading to irreversible damage or even death. Once the bleeding starts, it's almost impossible to stop. My mother passed away due to the same condition," he revealed, his voice tinged with pain.

He paused, looking down at his cappuccino. "If I had known then what I know now, I could have saved her. I watched her die, Saraswathi. That memory haunts me. I wish I could turn back time."

His eyes, glossy with unshed tears, betrayed the depth of his sorrow. Saraswathi remained quiet, offering him a moment of silent empathy as he got up from his chair to compose himself.

Though they lived in different parts of Minnesota—Dr. Deep in Mountview and Dr. Saraswathi in Shoreview—the two doctors shared a unique camaraderie. They worked seamlessly together in the hospital and found solace in each other's company outside work. Weekends, when free of emergencies, were often spent exploring the natural beauty of Minnesota.

One of their favorite spots was Lake Superior, one of North America's largest freshwater lakes. Sitting on its tranquil banks, they would watch the expansive water stretch toward Canada, dotted with large ships and vibrant wildlife. Children played with mallards and great blue herons while tourists wandered the lanes lined with Cedar trees.

During these moments, they indulged in simple pleasures—sharing a plate of Chipotle and sipping a bottle of Coke—before heading back to their respective homes. These quiet, rejuvenating outings became a ritual for the two, offering a much-needed respite from their demanding lives.

Saraswathi, ever introspective, chronicled these moments in her diary. Writing was therapeutic for her, allowing her to reflect on her experiences and emotions. Above all, she shared every detail of her life with her mother, Parvatakka, her closest confidante. There were no secrets between them, and Saraswathi's letters to her mother were filled with her joys, challenges, and even her budding connection with Dr. Deep.

Through these exchanges, the bond between Saraswathi and Deep deepened. Yet, neither had defined their relationship, choosing instead to let it evolve naturally. In their shared moments of vulnerability, laughter, and quiet understanding, they found a connection that both soothed and strengthened them.

Deep and Saraswathi decided to take a much-needed break and embarked on a road trip to Duluth City. Deep drove them in his sleek new Toyota Louis, and the three-hour journey promised a refreshing escape. Along the way, they stopped at a resting area surrounded by lush greenery. Deep looked dashing in his navy-blue T-shirt and grey pants, exuding an effortless charm. Saraswathi couldn't help but think how fortunate the woman who married Deep would be—a brilliant doctor and an equally remarkable human being.

From her bag, Saraswathi unpacked a box of freshly made **rava idlis** accompanied by coconut chutney and tangy pickle. Deep savored every bite, clearly enjoying the homemade meal. Then, Saraswathi pulled out a flask of coffee from Sagar Coffee House, her favorite. As she opened it, the rich aroma wafted through the serene forest, blending perfectly with the fresh air.

Duluth was breathtaking at this time of year, during the transitional beauty of September-October. The trees, including maple, ash, oak, and tamarack, were slowly preparing for winter. Their leaves transformed from deep green to golden and lemon-yellow before shedding entirely, leaving the branches bare but elegant. This enchanting metamorphosis was a sight to behold, a quiet miracle of nature. Deep admired the scenery but found himself gazing even more intently at Saraswathi.

She sat gracefully under the shade of a Jack pine tree, dressed in a champak-colored kurta and lavender semipatiala. Her presence was mesmerizing, and Deep couldn't stop stealing glances at her. At one point, he broke the silence with a heartfelt confession. "You look so pretty today, Saraswathi. Beautiful. If my mom were alive, she would have been so happy to see you."

Saraswathi's cheeks flushed, and she lowered her gaze, blushing at his words.

Saraswathi had always been passionate about music, a talent nurtured from her childhood. She had regularly performed speeches and musical pieces at school and college events. Just last month, at the **Minneapolis Kannada Koota**, she sang Dr. Shivarudrappa's poignant song, **"Ello Hudukide Illada Devara..."** Her soulful performance earned widespread applause. Deepak Pai and his wife, who had accompanied Saraswathi to the event, expressed their pride, telling her she was representing Karnataka on an international stage.

Deep had also attended the event at her invitation. Seeing Saraswathi in a traditional Kolkata cotton saree with a grand border, adorned with a large bindi on her forehead, her neatly woven hair cascading down, and her radiant smile, left him awestruck. She exuded grace and elegance, a stark yet delightful contrast to the casual attire he usually saw her wear—jeans and pullovers. That evening, Saraswathi resembled her namesake, the goddess of wisdom and beauty, **Devi Saraswathi.**

Deep sat speechless, captivated by her aura. Though he had always admired her, something about that evening deepened his appreciation, as if he had seen a new dimension to the Saraswathi he thought he knew. Their bond had always been meaningful, but moments like these made it feel extraordinary.

* * *

Sam's gratitude toward Dr. Deep and Dr. Saraswathi was boundless. "My son is alive and standing in front of me today only because of you both. I have no words to thank you. You gave my son another life, and I shall always remain indebted to you," he often said. Deep and Saraswathi humbly replied, "We just did our job, Mr. Sam. Thank you for trusting us."

Having entrusted the family's real estate business to his son Robert, Sam decided to retire with his wife to Santiago. On weekends, Robert would visit them and take them on drives in his sleek Cadillac. But what surprised everyone was the profound change in Robert's outlook on life after his interactions with Dr. Deep and Dr. Saraswathi. Their compassion, dedication, and values deeply influenced Robert, sparking in him a newfound appreciation for Indian culture and principles.

As time passed, Saraswathi began to notice changes in her own behavior. Her happiness seemed to revolve around the time she spent with Deep. She found herself missing him dearly during a week-long trip he took to New Jersey, and an unexpected pang of jealousy surfaced when she learned that Dr. Priscilla had accompanied him. She tried to rationalize her discomfort when she saw Priscilla attempting to get close to Deep. But Saraswathi's unease eased when she realized Deep didn't reciprocate Priscilla's advances. True to his composed and respectful nature, Deep maintained a professional demeanour, earning himself the playful nickname "Freeze" from Priscilla before she finally moved on. This incident reassured Saraswathi of her special bond with him.

One evening, during a phone call with her mother, Saraswathi decided to broach the subject of her feelings. "Aayi, will you give your consent if I want to marry Deep?" she asked, her voice tinged with both hope and anxiety. When Parvatakka remained silent for a moment, Saraswathi pressed on, "Did you hear me, Aayi? I love him."

"Yes, my daughter, I heard you," replied Parvatakka gently. "You can marry him, but only if he loves you as deeply as you love him. But remember this—don't give yourself to him physically before he confesses his feelings and agrees to marry you."

Saraswathi couldn't help but laugh at her mother's advice, finding it both amusing and endearing. "You sound like something out of a Charlie Chaplin book, Aayi," she teased, recalling similar advice in one of the comedian's writings. "Oh! My mother's life is almost as dramatic as Chaplin's," she thought to herself, chuckling.

Parvatakka's own life had been filled with trials. She married late, at the age of 30, as her focus had always been on her nursing career and serving people. Her happiness, however, was short-lived. Her husband, Subbaraya, passed away from a cardiac arrest just two years into their marriage. Parvatakka, already a mother to Saraswathi by then, found solace in her daughter and dedicated her life to raising her. Despite the hardships, she never allowed loneliness to overtake her, channeling her energy into her work and her devotion to her community. Her resilience became a source of strength and inspiration for Saraswathi, who admired her mother's ability to overcome life's challenges with grace.

Saraswathi listened intently as Deep began to share his story. She could sense the depth of emotion behind his words, the weight of memories he carried silently until now.

"In Chittapur," Deep continued, "we have this ancestral home, a sprawling but aging structure overlooking the Hooghly River. It has an air of history about it, much like the places my father spent his life studying. My father, Dr. Dhananjay Chatterjee, retired as the Director of the Archaeological Department. His world revolved around ancient ruins, inscriptions, and forgotten temples. He was always in search of stories etched in stone."

Deep paused for a moment, his gaze fixed on the distance as if replaying moments from his past. "My father married young, but his career kept him on the move. His work often took him to remote corners of the country, leaving my mother to stay with my grandparents back in Chittapur. For as long as I can remember, he lived a solitary life, even when we were a family. I rarely saw him, and the times I did, he seemed more like a visitor than a father."

Saraswathi leaned in, her curiosity growing. "That must have been hard for you and your mother," she said softly.

Deep nodded. "It was, especially for my mother. She was a beautiful soul, full of warmth and kindness, but loneliness etched deep lines into her face. She devoted herself to raising me, ensuring I had the best education and values, despite everything. She wanted to keep our family together, even if it meant bearing the brunt of my father's absence.

"As for me," Deep said, a faint smile forming on his lips, "I found solace in books and studies. My mother always said that learning could be my escape, my refuge. She was right. Medicine became not just a career for me but a purpose—a way to bring light into lives dimmed by darkness. And maybe, in a way, I was trying to do what I couldn't do for her when she fell ill."

Saraswathi reached out and placed her hand gently over Deep's. "You've carried so much in your heart," she said, her voice filled with understanding. "But you've turned it into something beautiful. You've become someone your mother would be so proud of."

Deep looked at her, his eyes softening. "Saraswathi, my mother's death was the turning point in my life. She suffered from an aneurysm, and it claimed her before we could even realize the severity of it. I've always carried the regret of not being able to save her. That's why I chose neurosurgery—why I dedicate myself completely to every patient who comes to me. It's my way of honoring her memory."

Saraswathi's eyes welled up as she listened to Deep's story. "You've done more than honor her memory," she said. "You've brought hope and life to so many people. Your mother would be so proud of the man you've become."

Deep smiled faintly, the heaviness in his heart easing for the first time in years. "Thank you, Saraswathi," he said. "Sharing this with you feels like lifting a weight I've carried for too long."

In that moment, as the cool breeze from the Hooghly River seemed to brush past them despite their distance from it, Saraswathi and Deep felt an unspoken bond deepen. They both knew their lives had been shaped by pain and resilience and now, perhaps, they had found solace in each other.

Saraswathi listened to Deep with a mixture of empathy and admiration. She could see the pain and conflict etched into every word he spoke. Deep's vulnerability revealed a side of him she hadn't seen before—a man who carried not only the weight of his profession but also the unresolved emotions of his past.

Deep continued, his voice softer now, "I've spent so much of my life trying to understand my father, but maybe some things are just not meant to be understood. My mother deserved so much more than she got, and yet she never spoke ill of him. She always said, 'Your father is a man of few words, but he has his own way of showing love.' I never believed her then, but now, when I think about those trips to KC Das and the rasagullas, I wonder if she was right. Maybe he loved us in his own quiet, flawed way."

Saraswathi leaned closer, her hand resting gently on Deep's. "Deep, you've done so much with the pain you've carried. You've turned it into a purpose, into a way of helping others. That's remarkable. But maybe it's time to find some peace with your father. You said he's alone now. Perhaps bringing him here to the US isn't just for him; maybe it's for you too. To try to bridge the gap."

Deep looked at her, the weight of her words sinking in. "You might be right," he admitted. "I've been holding onto resentment for so long that I've never given myself—or him—a chance to heal.

Maybe it's time to let go of the past and try to create something new."

Saraswathi smiled, her eyes reflecting warmth and encouragement. "You've already taken the hardest step, Deep—acknowledging the pain and wanting to do something about it. The rest will follow."

Deep chuckled softly, wiping the tears that had escaped his eyes. "You know, Saraswathi, I've always been so focused on fixing things for others—my patients, their families—but I never realized I needed fixing too. Thank you for listening, for being here."

Saraswathi squeezed his hand. "That's what friends are for, Deep. And maybe more than friends," she added with a playful smile, trying to lighten the mood.

Deep smiled back, a rare glimmer of hope breaking through the somberness. For the first time in a long time, he felt a sense of possibility—not just for his relationship with his father but for himself and for the connection he was building with Saraswathi.

The two sat there in companionable silence for a while, the weight of the past giving way to the hope of the future. It wasn't just about Deep's journey anymore; it was about the bonds he was beginning to forge—both old and new.

Parvatakka greeted Dr. Dhananjay with a warm smile and folded hands, saying, "Namaste." She looked serene in her white saree, her presence exuding a calm and motherly vibe. Dhananjay couldn't help but notice how gracefully she carried herself.

"Namaste, Madam," Dhananjay responded. "I hear a lot about your famous Karnataka cuisine. I look forward to tasting it."

Parvatakka chuckled lightly. "You must try everything, Uncle. I have brought enough to last a month!" she said, unpacking jars of homemade snacks and powders.

The dinner table was soon filled with dishes like *holige*, *kosambari*, *bisi bele bath*, and *chitranna*, all prepared by Parvatakka and Saraswathi. The aroma filled the house, bringing a nostalgic smile to everyone's face. As they all sat down to eat, the atmosphere became lighthearted and familial.

Over dinner, Saraswathi and Deep shared stories about their work, their first surgeries together, and how their friendship had evolved over time. Parvatakka listened intently, often chiming in with her wisdom, while Dhananjay occasionally glanced at Parvatakka with a curious expression, as if still trying to place her in his memory.

"You know, Madam," Dhananjay finally said, addressing Parvatakka, "I feel like I've met you before. Your face is so familiar."

Parvatakka looked up from her plate and smiled. "Well, Doctor, perhaps in another lifetime!" she joked, brushing it off with laughter.

Saraswathi watched the exchange and noticed something different in Dhananjay's expression—a flicker of recognition, maybe even admiration. She decided not to dwell on it and focused on making sure everyone was enjoying the meal.

A Growing Bond

Over the following days, Parvatakka and Dhananjay began spending more time together during their outings with Saraswathi and Deep. They discussed everything from Indian philosophy to family values. Parvatakka's warmth and wisdom seemed to draw Dhananjay out of his usually reserved demeanor. He found himself opening up about his past, his regrets about not being a better husband, and the loneliness he carried with him after his wife's passing.

"You know, life doesn't give us second chances, Parvatakka," Dhananjay said one day as they strolled through a park. "But seeing how you've faced your struggles with such grace—it's inspiring. I've been so lost in my own world of books and work that I've forgotten how to truly live."

Parvatakka smiled gently. "We all carry our burdens, Doctor. But it's never too late to find peace. Relationships heal when we give them our time and effort. Perhaps this visit is a chance for you to reconnect—with your son and even with yourself."

Dhananjay nodded thoughtfully, her words resonating deeply with him. He glanced at Deep and Saraswathi, walking ahead of them, laughing and sharing stories. A quiet sense of hope stirred within him.

An Unexpected Connection

One evening, as Parvatakka prepared *raagi mudde* and *sambar*, Dhananjay finally remembered where he had seen her before. It was during a medical camp he had attended in Karnataka decades ago. She had been volunteering as a nurse, tirelessly helping patients, her compassion leaving a lasting impression on him.

"Madam," he said, his voice filled with newfound excitement, "I know where I've seen you. You were at the medical camp in Chikkamagaluru, weren't you? I remember how selflessly you worked there."

Parvatakka looked surprised but nodded. "Yes, I volunteered there for years. But that was so long ago! It's amazing that you remember."

"I never forget acts of kindness," Dhananjay said with a smile. "Perhaps it's fate that our paths have crossed again."

From that moment, a deep respect blossomed between the two. Their shared experiences and mutual understanding brought a sense of companionship that neither had expected.

A New Beginning

As the days passed, Deep and Saraswathi noticed the growing bond between their parents. It was heartening to see them share laughs, stories, and even quiet moments of reflection. For Deep, it was a side of his father he hadn't seen in years—a man who was willing to step out of his shell and connect with others. For Saraswathi, it was comforting to see her mother finding a friend in Dhananjay.

On the last evening of their vacation, as they all sat around a bonfire by Lake Superior, Dhananjay spoke up. "This trip has been more than just a vacation for me. It's been a journey of healing and rediscovery. Thank you, Parvatakka, for reminding me what it means to live with purpose and grace."

Parvatakka smiled warmly. "And thank you, Doctor, for reminding me that even in our later years, life has surprises in store."

Deep and Saraswathi exchanged a knowing glance, their hearts full as they watched their parents embrace the possibility of new beginnings. It was a moment of connection, hope, and love—proof that even across polarities, hearts could meet and heal.

The day of the wedding was one of the most joyous and emotional moments for everyone. Saraswathi and Deep stood at the altar, their eyes filled with love and a sense of completeness. The ceremony was a fusion of traditions, honoring both their Indian roots and the life they had built in America. Guests from all walks of their lives—friends, colleagues, and family—gathered to witness their union.

Parvatakka wore a beautiful saree gifted by Saraswathi, her face glowing with happiness as she blessed her daughter and Deep. Dr. Dhananjay, dressed in a traditional dhoti and kurta, stood beside Parvatakka, the two sharing a bond of unspoken understanding. It was a moment of redemption for him, a chance to relive what he had lost years ago, this time through his son's happiness.

Sam and his wife attended the wedding as proud and grateful friends, their hearts full as they watched Deep and Saraswathi begin their new life together. Sam handed over the deed to the Mountview house as a gift, saying, "You two saved my son's life, and now you're building one together. This house is my way of saying thank you, though it could never match what you've done for us."

A New Chapter

Deep and Saraswathi moved into the Mountview house, creating a home filled with love, laughter, and shared dreams. They often hosted gatherings, bringing together their parents and friends, merging cultures and experiences. Parvatakka and Dr. Dhananjay found a newfound camaraderie, spending hours discussing literature, philosophy, and their memories of India.

On weekends, Deep and Saraswathi would take their parents to explore Minnesota's beautiful landscapes. They visited the Duluth shores again, this time as a family, marveling at how life had brought them all together.

Saraswathi continued her tradition of recording her thoughts in her diary, often writing about how love had transformed not only her life but also her mother's. Deep, on the other hand, started writing a memoir about his journey from Kolkata to Minnesota, dedicating a chapter to his mother and Parvatakka, whose resilience had inspired him to be the man he had become.

Healing the Past

Dhananjay opened up more as time passed, sharing stories of his youth and his regrets. He apologized to Parvatakka one evening, saying, "I should have returned, Parvathi. I failed you, and for that, I will always be sorry."

Parvatakka placed her hand on his and replied, "Dhananjay, life is too short for regrets. What matters is that we are here now, witnessing our children create a life we could only dream of. That is enough for me."

Full Circle

Saraswathi and Deep's wedding and life together symbolized a bridge between past and present, a second chance not just for their parents but for everyone involved. They carried forward the dreams and sacrifices of their families, proving that even the most broken paths could lead to beautiful destinations.

As Parvatakka watched her daughter and son-in-law grow together, she often whispered a prayer of gratitude, thanking destiny for bringing her long-lost love back into her life in an unexpected yet fulfilling way. For her, the story had not ended—it had simply taken a beautiful turn, one that she cherished with every beat of her heart.

10

THE DENIAL

Shripad's silent grief moved the entire gathering. The villagers, who had gathered to pay their respects, whispered among themselves, their voices filled with empathy and admiration. They understood the depth of his pain, having lost his only remaining connection to his childhood, his roots, and the woman who had been the backbone of his life.

The Legacy of Gaurakka

Gaurakka's life was not ordinary. Beyond being a teacher, she had been a beacon of hope and a mother figure to many in the village. She had set up literacy camps for women, initiated self-help groups, and even facilitated loans for young farmers through her connections. Her work extended beyond education, as she had actively helped the village modernize while preserving its traditional values.

The foundation she had started—**Gaurakka Seva Samithi**—was known for sponsoring the education of underprivileged children and supporting widowed women with skill development. Shripad had taken her legacy seriously, continuing to fund the foundation even after moving to the US. The villagers were deeply grateful for everything Gaurakka had done, and her death felt like the end of an era for the entire community.

The Day of Samaradhane

The **Vaikunta Samaradhane** was a grand affair. Shripad had spared no expense, ensuring that his mother's farewell reflected her stature and the love she had shared with everyone. The entire hall, **Sri Keshav Chandrashala**, was decorated with strings of marigold and jasmine. Traditional **rangoli** patterns adorned the entrance. Large pots of steaming **bisibele bath**, **kesari bath**, **holige**, and other Karnataka delicacies were being served by volunteers from the village.

Shripad's relatives, along with the elders of the village, performed the rituals with reverence. The priests chanted Sanskrit hymns, creating an atmosphere that resonated with both grief and spiritual solace.

The Moment of Denial

As Shripad sat amidst the crowd, he overheard some murmurs from a group of elderly men.

"This is Shripad's life now—a modern man in the US. He may not return again. Will he come back to look after Gaurakka's foundation?" one of them whispered.

Another replied, "He's already so detached from the village. You can't expect him to maintain her legacy."

Shripad clenched his fists as he heard these words. He wanted to stand up and shout that this was not true, that he had always been connected to his roots and had never forgotten his mother's teachings. But his emotions choked him, and all he could do was hold back tears.

After the rituals, Shripad approached Gappati. "What do you think they're saying, Gappati? Do they think I've forgotten this village? Do they think I'll abandon everything my mother built?"

Gappati placed a comforting hand on his shoulder and said, "Shripad, people talk because they don't know the truth. Your actions will speak louder than their words. Your mother's soul knows your intentions, and that's what matters."

A Renewed Purpose

That evening, Shripad sat alone in the temple hall, surrounded by the faint aroma of the incense sticks and the lingering echoes of the day's chants. He made a silent vow:

"I will not let my mother's work fade into oblivion. This village is my home, no matter where I live. Her foundation, her dreams, her people—they will remain a part of me."

A New Chapter

A few weeks later, Shripad initiated a plan to expand **Gaurakka Seva Samithi**. He announced scholarships for village students to study abroad, healthcare camps for the elderly, and financial aid for widowed women. He also began making arrangements to visit the village more often, ensuring that he could personally oversee the work.

As word spread about Shripad's commitment, the same people who had doubted him began to admire his dedication. They realized that Gaurakka's teachings had shaped him into the man he was—strong, compassionate, and deeply rooted in his culture.

The Legacy Continues

Shripad became a bridge between two worlds—the traditional life of the village and the modernity of the West. His mother's life and sacrifices had not gone in vain. As he carried forward her work, he also found peace, knowing that he was fulfilling her dreams.

And in the quiet moments of his busy life, whenever he looked at the foundation's achievements or the smiling faces of the villagers, he felt his mother's presence. Gaurakka was gone, but her legacy lived on, shining brightly in the lives she had touched and in the heart of her son, who now walked the path she had paved.

Shripad was taken aback by his uncle's harsh response. He had expected some hesitation or questions, but the outright rejection was a blow he hadn't anticipated. Shripad's confidence wavered, but he composed himself.

"Uncle, I understand that you have high aspirations for Vidya, and I respect that. But I must say, no one knows Vidya as I do. We've grown up together. It's not just about education or career; it's about understanding, trust, and mutual respect. I can promise you that I'll keep her happy and ensure she has everything she needs to thrive."

Rama Jois cut him off sharply. "Shripad, you may have grown up with her, but that doesn't make you the right match for her. Vidya deserves someone who can elevate her life, someone who fits into the vision I have for her future. You are a lawyer, and I do not mean to disrespect your profession, but it's not what I want for Vidya. This discussion is over."

Gaurakka, who had been quietly observing the exchange, stepped in. "Rama, Shripad has approached you with respect and genuine intentions. At least consider what he's saying. Vidya and Shripad share a bond that most couples spend years trying to build. Isn't that worth something?"

But Rama Jois was unmoved. "Gauri, I understand your sentiments, but my decision is final. I have already given my word to Somayaji's family. Vidya will be married to his son in three months. Please don't bring this up again."

Shripad clenched his fists, feeling both anger and helplessness. He knew his uncle was a man of rigid principles, but he hadn't expected this level of resistance. He looked at Vidya, who had been standing silently in the corner of the room, her head bowed.

"Vidya, do you have nothing to say?" Shripad asked, his voice trembling.

Vidya hesitated, glancing nervously between her father and Shripad. Finally, she spoke, her voice barely audible. "Shripad, I… I can't go against my father's wishes. He's always made decisions for me, and I trust him. Please understand."

Her words felt like a dagger to Shripad's heart. He had hoped she would stand up for their bond, but her silence and compliance shattered him.

Gaurakka, sensing her son's pain, placed a comforting hand on his shoulder. "Let's go, Shripad," she said softly. "There's nothing more to say here."

As they walked out of the house, Shripad felt a wave of emotions—anger, sadness, and a deep sense of betrayal. He couldn't understand how years of friendship and trust could be dismissed so easily.

Back home, Shripad locked himself in his room. He replayed the conversation with his uncle over and over in his mind, trying to make sense of it. His mother knocked on the door and entered, bringing him a glass of water.

"Shripad, I know you're hurt," she said gently. "But sometimes, life doesn't go the way we want it to. You've done your part by expressing your feelings. Now, you must learn to let go."

Shripad looked at his mother, his eyes filled with pain. "How can I let go, Amma? Vidya wasn't just my cousin; she was my best friend, my confidant. And now, I'm supposed to watch her marry someone else?"

Gaurakka sighed. "Life tests us in ways we don't expect, Shripad. But remember, your worth isn't determined by someone else's decision. You have a bright future ahead of you. Focus on that, and let time heal your wounds."

Despite his mother's comforting words, Shripad felt a void that refused to be filled. Over the next few weeks, he threw himself into his work, trying to distract himself from the pain. But every now and then, memories of Vidya would creep in, reminding him of what could have been.

On the day of Vidya's wedding, Shripad stayed home. He couldn't bring himself to attend, knowing it would be too painful.

Instead, he sat in his mother's room, reminiscing about the moments they had shared.

Though the pain eventually dulled with time, the experience left an indelible mark on Shripad's heart. It taught him about the harsh realities of societal expectations and the strength it took to move forward in the face of denial.

The next morning, Vidya arrived at Shripad's house. The morning air was cool, and a light mist lingered over the village. Shripad was seated on the veranda, sipping a cup of steaming coffee, his face calm but contemplative. He motioned for Vidya to join him.

"Vidya, sit down," he said, his voice steady but gentle. "There's something I want to talk about."

Vidya sat beside him, holding a small stainless steel container of halu obbattu (milk sweet roti) she had prepared as an offering. The aroma of the freshly made sweet wafted through the air, but Shripad didn't seem to notice.

"I've heard from Gappati about your situation," Shripad began. Vidya looked away, her face betraying a mixture of sadness and discomfort. "You don't have to explain or justify anything to me. I know how life can take turns we don't anticipate. I've had my fair share of those."

Vidya's eyes filled with tears. "Shripad, I didn't want my life to turn out this way. I thought I was doing the right thing by agreeing to my father's wishes. But not a single day passed where I didn't wonder if I made the biggest mistake of my life."

Shripad remained silent, letting her speak.

"My marriage was everything my father wanted—on paper. A scientist husband, a life in London, and respectability. But in reality, it was cold, distant, and lifeless. He never cared about me, Shripad. To him, I was just someone who had to fit into his routine, a tick on his list of expectations. And when things fell apart, there was no one to turn to."

Shripad listened intently, his gaze fixed on the distant horizon. He let her words hang in the air for a moment before responding.

"Vidya, I was angry and hurt back then—not because of your decision, but because of how it unfolded. I never blamed you. Life put us on different paths, but here we are again, at the same crossroads. Maybe it's fate, or maybe it's just time."

Vidya's eyes widened as she looked at him. "Do you mean that, Shripad? After everything, do you still think we could...?"

Shripad cut her off gently. "Vidya, we're not the same people we were back then. Life has shaped us, for better or worse. But what hasn't changed is the bond we've always shared. If we still feel the same way, maybe we should stop fighting it."

Vidya wiped a tear rolling down her cheek and managed a small smile. "You're right, Shripad. Life has given us a second chance, and I don't want to let it slip away."

Shripad reached out and held her hand, a quiet determination in his eyes. "Then let's make this work, Vidya. Let's not let the past dictate our future. This time, it's our decision."

The two sat in silence for a while, their hands intertwined, as the sun rose higher in the sky, casting its golden glow over the village. It felt as though the weight of years had been lifted from their shoulders.

Later that day, Shripad and Vidya informed their families about their decision. Gappati was overjoyed, and Vidya's mother, though initially hesitant, gave her blessings. Shripad's relatives, too, supported the decision, seeing it as a fitting conclusion to a story that had spanned decades.

In the weeks that followed, the preparations for Shripad and Vidya's wedding began. The event was to be a simple, traditional ceremony at the newly renovated Sri Keshav temple—an ode to Gaurakka's memory and the legacy of their shared heritage.

On the wedding day, as Shripad and Vidya stood before the sacred fire, surrounded by family and friends, it felt as though the pieces of their lives had finally fallen into place. Their journey, though fraught with obstacles, had brought them back to where they belonged—together.

As the flight soared through the clouds, Shripad's thoughts spiraled deeper into the past. Memories of his childhood with Gaurakka resurfaced like pages flipping through an old photo album.

He remembered the modest yet warm house they lived in after moving out of his father's property. Gaurakka would wake up before dawn every day, prepare breakfast, and pack Shripad's lunch before heading to the school where she worked as a teacher. Despite her meager income, she made sure Shripad never felt the absence of luxuries his classmates had. She took up extra tuition classes in the evenings and stitched clothes for neighbors to make ends meet. Shripad's heart ached as he remembered her hands—rough from years of hard work yet gentle whenever she caressed his face or patted his back in encouragement.

At Dharwad University, Shripad excelled in his law studies. He often called Gaurakka to share his achievements, and every time she would say, "Shripad, your success is my victory. Make your mother proud." Those words became his mantra, pushing him through the toughest of times.

However, life was not kind to Shripad's mother. She faced criticism and taunts from relatives who questioned her independence and her decision to raise Shripad on her own. But Gaurakka was resilient. She brushed aside societal judgment and focused entirely on building a life for her son. "You are my legacy, Shripad," she often said, her eyes brimming with hope.

The flight's turbulence jolted Shripad back to the present. He stared at the small, untouched salad in front of him. A tear slipped down his cheek as he recalled their last meal together. Just the previous evening, Gaurakka had fried Bondas with her own hands, insisting, "Shripad, you work so hard. Let your mother spoil you for a while." He had teased her for overcooking the Bondas, and she had laughed, saying, "Next time, I'll make them perfect." Little did he know that there would never be a next time.

He clenched his fists as he thought of the sacrifices she made for him. Her relentless dedication had enabled him to build a successful career in law and settle in the US. He wanted to give her the world in return. He had planned to take her on trips to Europe, show her the Eiffel Tower she always admired in magazines, and let her experience the joys she had been denied. But time had cruelly snatched that opportunity away.

As the flight neared Bengaluru, Shripad whispered to himself, "You deserved so much more, Amma. I wish I could have given you the life you deserved." He took a deep breath, vowing to honor her legacy by continuing the charitable work she had begun.

Upon landing in Bengaluru, Shripad felt a pang of reality hit him. The coffin carrying his beloved mother was carefully unloaded and handed over to him. A group of close relatives, led by Gappati, waited to receive him at the airport. Seeing their somber faces, Shripad struggled to hold back his tears.

As they drove to the hall, he saw the village preparing for Gaurakka's final rites. Her former students, colleagues, and countless people whose lives she had touched had gathered to pay their respects. Shripad realized that his mother's influence had extended far beyond their family. She had left an indelible mark on the community.

As the procession began, Shripad held the garland meant for his mother's portrait. He promised her in his heart, "Amma, I will carry forward your spirit of service. Your life was an example of selflessness, and I will ensure it inspires others for generations to come."

The day of the Vaikunta Samaradhane arrived, and Shripad stood before the gathering, his voice steady despite the lump in his throat. "My mother was not just my Amma," he began, "She was a teacher, a guide, a warrior, and an angel who gave everything for others. Her love was my strength, and her values will remain my guiding light. Let us all remember her not with sadness, but with gratitude for the life she lived and the legacy she leaves behind."

Applause erupted, and amidst it, Shripad felt a small yet comforting presence within him—his mother, forever watching over him.

Shripad recalled his visit to London with vivid clarity as the memories came rushing back while he sipped his lemonade. He had been eager to see Vidya after so many years. Despite the rejection and the hurt it caused his mother, Shripad had buried the pain and kept his affection for Vidya as a cherished memory of their shared childhood.

Vidya met him at his hotel in a sleek black sedan. She looked radiant, dressed in a navy-blue coat and scarf that complemented her modern, confident persona. Her smile lit up the room as she exclaimed, "Shripad! It feels like a lifetime since we last saw each other."

Shripad smiled warmly. "Vidya, you haven't changed at all. Still the same—full of life."

She laughed. "And you, still the serious, studious Shripad I remember, but now with a suit and tie. So, tell me, Mr. Lawyer, how's life in America?"

They spent the evening catching up over tea at a quaint café near Oxford. Vidya shared stories about her life in London, her research work, and her little boy, Rishi. But as they talked, Shripad noticed a subtle sadness in her eyes—a shadow of something she wasn't saying.

"Vidya," he said gently, "is everything alright?"

She hesitated before replying, "Life is… different, Shripad. My marriage hasn't been easy. Things didn't turn out the way I imagined."

Shripad felt a pang of sympathy. He wanted to ask more but chose to respect her boundaries. Instead, he said, "If you ever need a friend, Vidya, you know where to find me."

Vidya smiled faintly. "Thank you, Shripad. That means a lot."

As the days passed, they spent more time together exploring the city. Vidya took Shripad to some of her favorite spots—Hyde Park, the British Museum, and a little Indian restaurant tucked away in a quiet street. It felt like old times, a bittersweet reminder of what could have been but also a celebration of the bond they still shared.

At the end of his trip, Vidya drove him to the airport. As they said their goodbyes, she hugged him tightly and whispered, "Take care, Shripad. And thank you for being here. It meant more than you know."

Shripad returned to the US with a mix of emotions. He was glad to have reconnected with Vidya, but her unhappiness lingered in his thoughts. He couldn't help but wonder if life would have been different had things worked out between them. Yet, he reminded himself that he had no regrets. He had made peace with the past and was proud of the life he had built for himself and his mother.

Back in the present, Shripad's thoughts shifted to Gaurakka. He realized that she had always been his anchor, the one who had given him strength through every storm. Her absence now left a void he knew he could never fill. But her teachings, her resilience, and her unconditional love would forever guide him.

As the car approached the hall, Shripad straightened up and took a deep breath. He had a duty to fulfill—to honor his mother's legacy and the sacrifices she had made. He stepped out of the car, ready to face the crowd and give Gaurakka the farewell she deserved. Her love and values would remain his guiding light, just as they always had.

Shripad looked at Vidya, puzzled by her sudden gesture. It wasn't like her to show such vulnerability. She had always been the strong, independent woman he knew from their childhood, but now there was a softness in her demeanor, an unspoken sadness that lingered between them. He squeezed her hand gently, offering silent support, knowing that perhaps there was more beneath the surface than she was letting on.

Vidya smiled faintly but quickly withdrew her hand, as if realizing the moment had become too intimate for comfort. She looked away toward the serene lake, the morning mist hanging over the water, its stillness reflecting her own internal turmoil.

"It's not about your remark, Shripad," she said after a long pause. "It's just that... things have changed between Vishwanath and me. Ever since I became pregnant, he's been distant. I think he's struggling with it, and it's affecting everything. I'm just trying to keep things together, but I don't know how much longer I can."

Shripad listened carefully, his concern deepening. He could sense the frustration and the uncertainty in her voice, but he didn't know how to help. His own life had been focused on his career and his mother, and now, in the wake of her passing, he was realizing how little he truly understood the complexities of relationships and the struggles of those close to him.

"You don't have to go through this alone, Vidya," Shripad said softly, his voice steady. "If you ever need to talk or just need someone to listen, I'm here."

Vidya turned to him, her eyes searching his face as if looking for something she couldn't quite name. "I know, Shripad," she said, her voice filled with a mixture of gratitude and sadness. "But I also know that we all have our own battles to face. You have your life, and I have mine. I just... I want things to work out, you know? For the sake of the baby. But I don't know if they will."

They stood there for a few more moments, in silence, watching the sunrise paint the sky in hues of pink and gold. The beauty of the moment seemed to contrast sharply with the heaviness in their hearts, but neither of them spoke of it again. Shripad knew there was little more he could do than to offer his support from afar, as he had always done, and Vidya, as always, would keep pushing forward, trying to make the best of things.

When it was time to leave, Shripad gave her a brief hug, an unspoken promise to be there whenever she needed him. As he walked away to catch his cab, Vidya stood at the bridge for a few moments longer, watching him go, unsure of where the future would take her, but knowing that at least for this moment, she had the support of an old friend.

As Shripad's cab disappeared down the winding road, Vidya turned back toward the lake, deep in thought. She didn't know what was going to happen with Vishwanath, or how she would navigate the challenges ahead, but she also knew that the memories of their childhood days and the friendship they shared would always remain a source of comfort for her.

* * *

Shripad was deeply moved by Vidya's words. He could feel the weight of her pain, and it pained him to see her in such a vulnerable state, yet still trying to make light of the situation. He had known Vidya since childhood, and the carefree, lively girl she once was seemed so far removed from the woman sitting before him now.

He looked at her with a mixture of sympathy and admiration. "Vidya, I never imagined you'd go through something like this. I'm so sorry for what you've endured. But I'm glad you're here now. You don't need to carry that burden anymore."

Vidya nodded, her eyes becoming distant for a moment before she snapped back to reality with a small, forced smile. "I don't want sympathy, Shripad. I want my life back. And I'm here, trying to figure out how to rebuild it. I don't want to wallow in my misery anymore, and I definitely don't want to become a bitter person because of him. But it's not easy, you know?"

Shripad sat up, now fully awake and focused on her. "Of course, it's not easy. But you're strong, Vidya. You've always been. You've got so much ahead of you, and you deserve peace. You deserve happiness again. And I'm here, for whatever you need."

Vidya looked at him, searching his face for sincerity, and she saw only honesty in his eyes. She let out a deep breath, as if carrying the weight of the last few years had left her physically drained.

"I know I've been through a lot, Shripad," she continued, "but I've never felt truly free until now. I've been stuck in that toxic relationship, feeling like I was suffocating. It took me so long to get the courage to leave, but I did it. And now, I have to start over, learn to trust again, learn to love again."

Shripad listened intently, not interrupting. He could tell this was not just about her divorce or her bruises; it was about reclaiming herself, rediscovering who she was outside of her past, and finding strength in the aftermath.

"You don't have to do it alone, Vidya," Shripad said quietly. "You've got me. And you've got yourself."

Vidya gave him a long look, and for the first time in months, she felt like she wasn't carrying the weight of the world on her shoulders. "Thank you, Shripad. That means more to me than you know."

They sat in silence for a while, the only sound being the distant hum of the city. Vidya glanced over at the window, where the sunlight streamed in, casting a warm glow across the room. For the first time, she felt like she might be able to see a future that was no longer clouded by fear and pain.

"Shripad," she said softly, her voice steady now, "I think... I think it's time I started living for myself. It's time to heal, and I'm ready to do that."

Shripad smiled, relieved to hear her speak with such determination. "I'm glad to hear that, Vidya. I know you'll find your way. And whatever that path looks like, I'll be right here."

Vidya stood up, walking over to the window, and Shripad followed her, standing beside her. They looked out together, knowing that the road ahead wouldn't be easy, but it was one they could face together.

The warmth of their childhood bond filled the room, as both Vidya and Shripad found themselves lost in laughter and tears, wrapped in the familiar comfort of their shared memories. The weight of past years, filled with pain and struggle, seemed to dissipate, replaced by the lightness of their playful, childlike connection. For a moment, it felt like nothing had changed, and the world outside the room faded away.

Vidya wiped the tears from Shripad's face, her laughter still ringing in the air, and said, "See? No need to take everything so seriously. Life has a funny way of unfolding itself."

Shripad took a deep breath, feeling the release of emotions he hadn't allowed himself to feel for so long. "You're right, Vidya. You've always known how to bring me back to earth."

As they sat back down, Shripad glanced at her son, now sitting quietly in her lap, observing his parents. Shripad's heart swelled with an unexpected sense of hope. The future still seemed uncertain, but the love and strength between them, and the shared commitment to healing and growing, gave him a sense of peace.

"I admire you, Vidya. You've always had such clarity," Shripad said softly. "Starting the Sanskrit Veda Vidyalaya—it's a beautiful vision. You're not just rebuilding yourself; you're creating something that will give back to others. It's a legacy."

Vidya smiled, her eyes filled with determination. "It's the only way I know how to heal, Shripad. It's not just about teaching; it's about reconnecting with what's been lost. We can't truly move forward if we don't understand where we come from."

Shripad nodded in agreement, realizing just how much she had changed. She was no longer the girl he had known, but someone who had found strength in the face of adversity, someone who was determined to create something meaningful out of her life. He, too, had changed, in ways he had yet to fully grasp.

"Let's make sure we're both there when that Vidyalaya opens," Shripad said with a smirk. "I'll come back to check on it, and you better have it running smoothly by then."

Vidya laughed, giving him a playful shove. "Deal. But only if you come back with truckloads of money, just like you promised."

As they shared another round of laughter, Shripad knew that the bond they shared had withstood everything life had thrown at them. The future was still uncertain, but for the first time in a long time, it felt like they could face whatever came next—together.

ABOUT THE AUTHOR

Mr. Suresh Hegde is a retired Personnel Officer at Karnataka Power Corporation, who, at the age of 73, continues to dedicate himself passionately to the literary field. After serving for 38 years in a Government Organization, he is now settled in Hubli, Karnataka. Throughout his career, he cultivated a deep love for writing short stories in Kannada, and many of his works have been published in leading journals. His exceptional literary talent has been a tremendous asset to the community.

A science graduate with a degree in Law, Mr. Hegde also holds postgraduate diplomas in two other subjects, reflecting his wide-ranging interests and intellectual curiosity. He is a resource person for several institutions, offering his expertise and knowledge to those in the field. As an All India Radio (AIR) artiste in Drama, he has a keen interest in Theatre Arts, where his inquisitiveness and passion continue to flourish. Additionally, he has a profound appreciation for Vachana Sahitya, which adds another layer to his rich literary pursuits.

Now enjoying a fulfilling retired life, Mr. Hegde is the proud father of two fine-profiled sons and remains actively engaged in his literary endeavors.